GINGERBREAD AT MOONGLOW

A Moonglow Christmas Novella

DEBORAH GARNER

CRANBERRY COVE PRESS

Cranberry Cove Press / Published by arrangement with the author

Gingerbread at Moonglow by Deborah Garner

Cranberry Cove Press
PO Box 1671
Jackson, WY 83001, United States

Library of Congress Catalog-in-Publication Data Available
Garner, Deborah
Gingerbread at Moonglow / Deborah Garner—1st United States edition
1. Fiction 2. Woman Authors 3. Holidays

p. cm.
ISBN-13:
978-0-9969960-3-7 (paperback)
978-0-9969961-0-5 (hardback)

Printed in the United States of America
10 9 8 7 6 5 4 3 2

GINGERBREAD AT
MOONGLOW

For my mother,
who always made holidays special for us.

And I had but one penny in the world,
thou shouldst have it to buy gingerbread.

William Shakespeare,
Love's Labour's Lost

Books by Deborah Garner

The Paige MacKenzie Mystery Series

Above the Bridge
The Moonglow Café
Three Silver Doves
Hutchins Creek Cache
Crazy Fox Ranch

The Moonglow Christmas Novella Series

Mistletoe at Moonglow
Silver Bells at Moonglow
Gingerbread at Moonglow
Nutcracker Sweets at Moonglow
Snowfall at Moonglow
Yuletide at Moonglow

The Sadie Kramer Flair Series

A Flair for Chardonnay
A Flair for Drama
A Flair for Beignets
A Flair for Truffles
A Flair for Flip-Flops
A Flair for Goblins

Cranberry Bluff

ONE

The enticing aromas of cinnamon, cloves, and honey floated across the kitchen as Mist removed a pan from the oven. She placed the freshly baked loaf on the stovetop, leaned slightly forward, and inhaled. Ah, yes, the touch of molasses she'd put into the batter made it more intense, just as she'd predicted. Experimenting with cooking was a major passion. Even a tiny substitution could change the overall experience of food.

Mist removed her oven mitts, handmade from scraps of favorite old clothes and padded with protective filling. She placed them on the kitchen counter and sat down to look over her notes. Not only had she written comments about each dish she'd tested over the past week, but she'd outlined the schedule for the next several days. Although it was her third year coordinating accommodations, meals, and activities for Christmas guests of the Timberton Hotel, this year promised to be challenging. Fortunately, Mist loved a good challenge. Since the hotel always had return guests for the holidays, along with new ones, Mist had to call on her creativity to be sure everything was different from previous years. This included decorations, menus, and tiny individual touches to the rooms. Mist had made plans months before, some even a year before, to accomplish this.

"Smells delicious!" Betty, the hotel innkeeper, entered the kitchen and made a beeline for the loaf now cooling on top of the stove. "What have you done with your culinary magic this time?" Betty breathed in the scent of spices.

"Better yet," a second voice said, "when can we test it out?" Clive Barnes, owner of the Timberton Gem Gallery, and Betty's beau, reached out to poke the loaf with his finger. Betty slapped his hand away while Mist watched the two with amusement.

"Clive," Betty scolded, "it's a well-known fact that you have appointed yourself the town's primary taste tester. But that doesn't mean you can go around poking every baked good as if it were the Pillsbury Doughboy. Your taste-tester role isn't official, you know."

Clive sat at the kitchen table, an island area where Mist, Betty, and Clive often met. He sighed. "Fine, then how about telling me what it is, and I'll try to wait patiently." He looked at Mist with an eager smile.

"Give it about ten minutes," Mist said as she transferred the loaf from the pan to a wire rack. "And it's a honey cake, basically, though I substituted a touch of molasses and added some lemon zest."

"Well, count me in when it's ready to be tested," Clive said. "Meanwhile, what does a guy have to do to get a cup of coffee around this place?" He winked at Mist, though he directed the comment to Betty, who tapped her finger to her forehead before answering.

"Let's see, Clive," Betty said. "You could do plenty of things for a cup of coffee. I think the front of the hotel could use a coat of paint. In fact, maybe primer first, then paint. And the trim… Let's see, there's that broken section on the west side…"

"Okay, I deserved that." Clive laughed. "I phrased my request poorly. I just may need a little caffeine to accomplish all that. Please."

Betty filled two mugs with coffee, set one in front of Clive, and sat down beside him with the other. Mist sipped the peppermint tea she'd already poured while she waited for the honey cake to finish cooling.

"We have a hectic week coming up," Betty said, looking at Mist almost apologetically. "We'll have more overnight holiday guests than usual this year, plus extra community activities. I'll help you as much as I can."

Mist reached over and squeezed Betty's hand. "Thanks, Betty. Your own workload is pretty heavy. I really think everything is under control though. We've been organizing for months. Maisie and Marge are both planning to be here during the special events. Maisie, of course, is bringing in all the floral goods through Maisie's Daisies. And Marge ordered plenty of candy through her candy store."

"You're certainly right about that," Betty said. "I saw UPS deliver a second shipment yesterday. Looked like enough to keep the whole town on a six-month sugar high."

"It will help that they won't be eating it all," Mist said. She stood, checked the honey cake, cut a slice for Clive, and placed it next to his coffee mug, much to his delight. Betty turned down a piece, citing she'd save it for dessert that night.

"Speaking of all that candy, Clive," Mist said. "How's the project coming along?"

"Delicious!" Clive said, taking a bite of the cake.

Mist tilted her head to the side, a dangling silver earring grazing her shoulder as she waited for a nonculinary answer.

"Oh, right, the project. It's coming along fine," Clive said. He eyed the cake with longing as if answering the question before taking another bite called on all his willpower. "I just need to add support beams for the roof, and it will be done. Clayton's going to help me bring it over in the morning."

"Well now, that's nice of Clayton to help out," Betty said. "He's got plenty on his hands this year, what with the new baby coming and all."

Mist smiled. She'd been thrilled when Clayton and Maisie had gotten married the previous spring and equally thrilled when Maisie announced at Thanksgiving that they were expecting. She'd watched the romance develop between the town's fire chief and the flower shop owner over the past couple of years. It warmed her heart to see two good people find each other.

"We'll need to bring it over in two sections," Clive said.

Betty looked back and forth between Mist and Clive, confused. "Why?"

"Well, Betty, it's like this..." Clive trailed off midsentence.

_____

4

"There was a slight misunderstanding," Mist offered. "But it's going to be fine. Once I realized the mix-up, I knew it was meant to be."

Betty drummed her fingers on the kitchen table. "We're talking about the gingerbread house decorating event, right?"

"Right," Mist and Clive both said.

"Clive has been helping with the model to get the dimensions right before you bake?"

Mist and Clive nodded.

"So… why would you need to bring it over in two sections? Didn't we decide on three by five? That's not very big, just the size of an index card."

"We ended up going with four by four," Clive said evasively. "Seemed a square shape would be good." He took another forkful of cake and popped it in his mouth as he and Mist exchanged looks.

"What am I missing here?" Betty said, clearly baffled. Mist knew she deserved an explanation. Or, perhaps better worded: a warning.

"I'll take the blame for this change in plans, Betty," Mist said. "I believe I didn't explain the specifics adequately to Clive. We had different… visions, it turned out. I think that's the best way to put it." She turned to Clive. "Wouldn't you agree?"

Clive swallowed, washed the bite of cake down with a sip of coffee, and looked up at Mist, grateful for her generous explanation. "Yes, different visions, a perfect way to put it."

"Well, I think four by four is just as good as three by five," Betty said. "I like the idea of square gingerbread

5

houses. That might even be better for people working at tables. But I still don't understand bringing the model over in two parts."

"Because of the front door," Clive said.

Mist held up her hand to Clive to show she would explain the rest. "Betty, I neglected to specify *inches* when I gave him the measurements." She waited while Betty processed the statement and watched as Betty's eyes grew wider. "So Clive made us something very unique."

"You can't mean…" Betty set her coffee mug down on the table.

Mist nodded. "Yes, we have a four *foot* by four *foot* gingerbread house model."

"Not four inches by four inches," Betty said. Her statement sounded more like a question, as if she'd heard incorrectly.

"Right. Feet, not inches," Mist said. "I think it will be grand, really I do." She paused, the odd thought striking her that she might sound a bit like Katherine Hepburn.

"But where will it go?" Betty now looked panic-stricken. She rose and began to pace the kitchen.

"In the front parlor," Mist said. "I have it figured out already."

"The front parlor?" Betty's concern was not abating. "That room isn't very big."

Betty had a good point, of course. When they'd added Mist's restaurant, Moonglow Café, to the hotel two years before, they'd used the larger of the two hotel parlors for its location. The smaller parlor still offered a comfortable sitting area for guests to lounge. But Clive's creation would certainly crowd it.

"I've measured the room carefully," Mist said, hoping to reassure Betty. "By placing the gingerbread house off-center, we'll still be able to keep the main couch area as it is. The Christmas tree will still be in the front window, the piano still in the front corner. We'll just move some of the furniture aside for the actual decorating, and then move it back."

Betty sighed, undoubtedly thinking of a different experience: cleaning up after what promised to be a chaotic series of events. It would help that the cookie exchange and the gingerbread house decorating would be at different times and wouldn't interfere with Christmas Eve dinner.

"Well, now that that's settled, I'm heading back to the gallery to finish up." Clive took his empty coffee mug and cake plate to the sink, kissed Mist's cheek and then Betty's as he said goodbye. He left through the kitchen's side door.

"My, my, my," Betty said to no one in particular. She absently touched her cheek where Clive had kissed her.

Mist reached over and patted Betty's hand. "It will be fine, you'll see. It will be a special Christmas."

"I don't doubt that in the least, Mist," Betty said. "You have a way of making the holidays magical. And you'll *need* a little magic to fit that gingerbread house in here with all the guests coming. Let me get the reservation book." She left the room briefly, returning with a large binder. Setting it on the table, she sat down while Mist flipped pages to the next day's date.

Normally, very little rattled Mist, but the timing of arrivals this year had her concerned. The first impression guests had of the hotel mattered, and she took pride in individualizing each person's experience. She wanted new guests to feel instantly welcomed and returning guests to feel like family. Her ideal would be to space arrivals an hour apart so that she could greet each person casually, make light conversation, escort guests to rooms, and find out if there was anything small she could offer to make them more comfortable. Rushed greetings felt impersonal.

"I don't know how we managed to have all the guests arriving on the same day this year," Betty said. "We've never had that happen before."

"It will work out," Mist said. "I just hope they spread out over a few hours." She ran her fingertips down the list of names, overhead lights bouncing off a flat turquoise ring on her thumb, a recent local thrift-store find.

"I think Clara and her 'special friend,' as she calls him, will be arriving first," Betty said. "Their plane gets into Bozeman early in the morning. I suspect they'll be here around noon."

Mist nodded. "That's what she said when I talked to her on the phone yesterday. She was worried it would be an inconvenience for us. Of course, I told her it wouldn't."

"She's such a sweet lady," Betty said. "I think she's nervous. It's a big step, bringing her new gentleman friend with her, after all those years coming here with Carl."

"I'm excited for her," Mist said. "She's been a widow for more than two years now. She deserves to be happy again. She won't be the only one bringing someone back with her, either. The English professor is bringing his sister and niece with him this year. They're going to be staying with him for a couple of months to help him settle in."

Betty nodded. "It's quite a transition for him, accepting a full-time job at the university where he guest lectured two years ago. He'll be house-hunting up in Missoula after the holidays. He sounded excited in his latest email."

"I'm sure the professor is nervous as well as excited," Mist said. "We'll need to make a point of easing his worries." Her fingers continued down the list, checking names room by room. "The Webers won't be here until later. That should be a lovely visit. They're bringing their newly adopted daughters."

"Oh, yes!" Betty exclaimed. I'm happy they've chosen the Timberton Hotel for their first Christmas together as an official family." She paused and then smiled wickedly. "But not everyone is bringing a companion. Isn't there someone you haven't mentioned yet, someone special?"

Despite her attempt to remain nonchalant, Mist blushed. Indeed one guest would be arriving alone. Knowing Betty's question was rhetorical, she simply smiled. It would be the third Christmas Michael Blanton would be with them at the hotel since Mist had arrived, and an attraction had been growing between them. Although Michael hadn't offered much of an explanation for why a proposed spring visit had fallen through, his emails had made it clear he was looking forward to seeing her. Mist trusted that their connection would remain strong even though she'd been disappointed.

"Well, then." Mist closed the registration book and stood, her work boots tapping the kitchen floor lightly. "The guests certainly won't all fit in that gingerbread house Clive is preparing for us. I'd better see to the rooms." Leaving Betty with her coffee, Mist returned the book to the registration desk and set to work on the guest accommodations.

TWO

The back hallway closet door creaked as Mist opened it and looked inside. She needed to remind Clive to oil it, or she'd do it herself when she had time. Multiple shelves held wooden bins, woven baskets, and various other containers, all filled with trinkets she acquired throughout the year that she could use to individualize the guest rooms. The assortments were odds and ends that she picked up whenever they struck her fancy. She collected the objects from the town thrift shop, Second Hand Sally's, as well as from local yard sales. She even made an occasional online discovery, though Mist rarely used a computer. She preferred to use her time painting or enjoying a cup of tea while she read.

Mist pulled a tin tub off one shelf and perused the contents: pewter jacks in a soft leather pouch, a miniature rocking horse, a cluster of skeleton keys, a terra cotta figurine of a pig, and several skeins of variegated yarn. She adored one skein in particular, finding its blue, green, and purple tones as soothing as the smooth texture of the yarn.

Replacing the tin tub, she lifted a wooden box off a different shelf and sat on the hallway floor, her soft rayon skirt folding around her in lavender ripples as she opened the lid. This had been one of her favorite discoveries at a recent craft fair in Helena. Not the box itself, though she was fond of that as well. She'd found it on the side of a road one day and sanded it down to a smooth finish. But the doilies inside were the real treasure. As she pulled them out one by one now, she thought back to the day she'd bought them. She'd sat for more than an hour with the elderly woman who'd made them, listening to the stories behind the designs. Each crocheted piece reflected a section of the woman's life—the birth of a child, the loss of a husband, a joyful reunion with a long-lost friend. The variety of shapes—round, square, oblong, haphazard—matched the mixed texture of life's emotions. Mist had left feeling honored to be able to take the doilies with her, knowing they would wordlessly share the woman's experiences with others.

A plastic case held another fortunate find at the same crafts fair. A young woman from Kalispell, in northern Montana, displayed a collection of handmade soaps with delightful, creative scents. Mist had fallen for the gentle, plant-based soaps on the spot, choosing several to bring back to the hotel: lemon chamomile, lavender oatmeal, and cinnamon clove.

Mist glanced around after closing the soap container and putting it up. Her wicker basket of fabric was filled to the brim with new scraps. And the collection of used books had grown over the past year as well. This was not only because Michael Blanton was such as avid reader but because Mist kept a variety of books in all the guest rooms. After all, on a vacation, someone usually absorbed with jobs, television, and the often overwhelming commotion of life, might discover the magic of reading simply by having the luxury of free time. There were supposed nonreaders in the world who loved to read, of that she was certain. They just didn't know it yet.

"Maisie's here with the flowers," Betty called from the end of the hallway. "What a spread you ordered this year! I'm running down to Marge's for a few minutes."

"Tell Maisie I'll be right out. And could you pick up some peppermint bark while you're getting your caramels?" Mist asked, a knowing grin crossing her face.

"How did you…? Oh never mind." Betty laughed. Her caramel cravings were legendary. She almost always had a few in her pocket, as well as a stash in a front desk drawer.

Before Mist closed the closet, she took the box with the doilies off the shelf again and hurried into each of the guests' rooms and suites, leaving a doily or two on dressers and nightstands, all different but connected by the hands and heart of the woman who crocheted them. She'd finish with the rooms later. She returned to the front of the hotel where she found Maisie in the hallway, three large buckets of flowers beside her and two butcher-paper wrapped groupings of greenery under her arms.

"Oh, Maisie." Mist sighed. "I'm sorry I kept you waiting even a little bit. You know I would have been happy to come down to your shop to pick everything up. Here, let me take those." She lifted the greenery from Maisie's arms and carried it into the café where the open tables could be used for projects between meals.

"I know," Maisie said, following Mist with one of the buckets. "But I needed to get out of the flower shop anyway. I've had such a rush of orders today, and I've had to turn many of them down. Four days before Christmas just isn't enough time to get what customers want. I hate disappointing people."

"You're not disappointing them, Maisie," Mist said as she retrieved the other two buckets of flowers from the hall. "They are disappointing themselves by not planning ahead."

"I suppose you're right," Maisie said, sitting. "And I always suggest other options even if they aren't exactly what they wanted at first." She shifted in her seat, trying to get comfortable.

Mist set the buckets down, gently pulled a chair from one of the tables, and positioned it opposite Maisie. She eyed it curiously from several angles. "That chair would look much better with feet on it, in my opinion," she said. "Don't you think so?"

Maisie smiled as she propped her feet up on the extra chair. "Thanks, Mist. It does help to keep my legs up." She leaned back, her usual work overalls snug against her expanding waistline.

"Wonderful," Mist said as she pulled a stalk from one of the buckets. "I wasn't sure you'd be able to get the winterberry holly stems, but these are perfect."

"I ordered them from a farm back in North Carolina, along with the birch branches mixed in with the greenery. Great new resource. I'll order from there again. I wouldn't have found them if you hadn't requested those berry stems. My usual vendors didn't have any."

Mist sorted through the mixed flowers, growing more excited as she pulled each variety out of the buckets. "The white parrot tulips are beautiful, and I love the paperwhites. You even found red Dendrobium—wonderful orchids, so different from the cymbidium we've used before."

"I was tempted to pick up some amaryllis," Maisie said, "in case you wanted more red. But you did say you wanted the focus to be on white flowers."

"What you brought is perfect," Mist said, placing the stems back in water. "We'll have plenty of color with the gingerbread house. I want to keep the rest of the decorations lighter in tone."

"Oh, how's that going? How many houses are you baking?" Maisie shifted her legs and settled back in the chair again.

"Well…" Mist sat down, moving a slender branch of boxwood tips aside, and rested her hands on the table, one on top of the other. "There's been a minor change in plans. As it turns out, we'll only be decorating one gingerbread house."

Maisie looked confused. "How can that work? Only so many people can fit around one table."

"True," Mist said. "But we won't be using a table. We'll be using a whole room, or a good part of one. You see, what happened was…"

The front door opened, cutting off Mist's explanation. Clive's voice followed.

"Just angle it toward the left, Clayton. That's it. Now keep moving forward, a little more, there you go."

Maisie and Mist watched as Clive's body appeared in the front entryway, followed by a large wood frame, followed by Maisie's husband.

Maisie's eyes grew wide. "What on earth... Clayton? Is this what you've been helping Clive with the past few days? I thought you two were working on a gingerbread house model?"

"Yep," Clayton said. "And this is it, half of it anyway." He set the edge of the half frame down. "We'll be right back with the other half." He paused and turned toward Maisie. "Hi ya, sweetheart, lookin' pretty."

Clive and Clayton left to make a second trip, leaving Maisie to look at Mist, eyebrows raised. "The other half?" she asked.

"There was a slight mix-up regarding the dimensions," Mist said calmly. She picked up a sprig of rosemary and inhaled, entertained by Maisie's bewildered expression.

Another door opened, this time the one leading from the kitchen.

"Candy, anyone?" Betty said, her voice singsong until she raised her eyes from the bag of candy and looked across the café into the entryway. "Oh my!"

"Beautiful flowers, aren't they?" Mist said impishly, knowing full well that Betty wasn't referring to Maisie's floral delivery.

Betty continued into the café and dropped into a chair, not noticing the piece of peppermint bark that fell from her bag onto a seeded eucalyptus branch. "It's big," she said.

"Four by four," Mist said.

"Four by four?" Maisie repeated.

"Without the roof," Mist clarified.

"Without the roof," Betty mused.

Clive and Clayton shuffled and thumped their way through the front door again, bringing the second half of the house, which they set down next to the first.

"We'll be back with the roof," Clive said.

"And the platform," Clayton added.

Maisie and Betty exchanged glances and both said, "The platform?"

Ten minutes later, all the pieces were in the front hallway. Thirty minutes after that, they were attached to each other: four walls, a sloped though shallow roof, and a low platform with wheels. Mist, Betty, and Maisie moved furniture aside in the front room, and Clive and Clayton rolled their creation in.

"It's kind of big," Clive said, scratching his head.

"It is big," Clayton agreed.

"It's so big," Maisie said.

"It's bigger than big," Betty said.

Mist approached the framed house, peeked in its doorway, tapped its roof, and walked around it twice. Finally she turned to face the others and clasped her hands, smiling.

"It's perfect," she said.

THREE

To keep the ovens free for baking thirty-two large slabs of gingerbread, Mist replaced Moonglow Café's normal, nightly gourmet meal with simpler fare, what might pass as lunch. When diners from town arrived, they found deluxe picnic offerings spread across the buffet: a tray of sourdough and multigrain breads, slices of honey-baked ham, turkey and roast beef, four types of cheese, hummus, avocado, tomato and crisp leaves of romaine lettuce large enough to make wraps for those who preferred to avoid bread. Small bowls of pickles, jalapeno peppers, onions, and radish sprouts sat to the side. A bowl of fresh pineapple and a platter of dark chocolate coconut bars rounded out the meal.

No one complained, and Mist was especially grateful that she could bake the twelve-by-twenty-four-inch cakes, along with a multitude of smaller rectangles to be used as shingles, through the dinner hour. The professional oven Clive had installed for the café allowed Mist to bake four panels at once. It would take many rounds of baking, but Maisie, a natural night owl, had offered to rotate some of the trays in at nighttime when Mist usually painted.

Her miniature paintings were selling well at Clive's gallery.

"What if some of these break when you move them from the racks?" Betty asked as she brought dinner plates into the kitchen to be washed.

"Then we'll fix them," Mist said. "Life is full of broken pieces that we can fix."

"That doesn't always work," Clive said. He sat down at the kitchen island with a sky-high concoction that appeared to have every item from the buffet inside two slices of bread.

"Good thing you have a big mouth on occasion, dear," Betty teased. "It'll help you tackle that sandwich."

Clive gave Betty a friendly swat as she left to collect more dishes, and then turned back to Mist. "Last time I broke something—a pitcher an artist friend made for me a long time ago—I had a tough time fixing it. I glued it back together, but it looked funny afterward."

"But it worked, didn't it?" Mist said.

"Yes, I guess so. I still use it." Clive took a hearty bite of his sandwich and contemplated Mist's statement while chewing.

"Fixing things doesn't always mean they'll be the same as they were before," Mist said. "Imperfections add variety—in objects, in people, in many things. Sometimes it's even fine for things to remain broken."

"If you say so, Mist." Clive bit into a dill pickle, resulting in a snap that made Mist smile.

"Do you think that pickle will taste worse, now that it's no longer whole?"

Clive looked at the pickle with mild curiosity. "No, I suppose not."

"Well, there you go," Mist said. She removed four trays of gingerbread from the oven, set them aside to cool, and replaced them with four waiting trays.

"I'll get the next four," Betty said as she returned to the kitchen. "And I'll clear the remaining dishes."

"Maisie offered to help, too, to give me some time to paint," Mist said.

"Good," Clive piped up, pickle finished. "You've got an order from a husband and wife who want two of the winterberry paintings."

"The order from yesterday?" Mist asked.

"No, a new one." Clive stood and carried his plate to the sink.

"All right," Mist said. "I can do four tonight." She looked at Betty. "Thank you for taking over the baking. It sounds like I'd better get to work."

"You know I'm happy to help," Betty said, shooing Mist out of the kitchen.

A short walk down the back hallway took Mist to her room, a peaceful space without the plumage of holiday décor that decked out the rest of the hotel. Simple furnishings filled the room, along with an easel and rack of paints. In one corner, a stack of cartons held small, framed canvases, approximately four inches by four inches, each one blank and waiting for an artist's handiwork. These would become miniature paintings to hang in Clive's gallery to spruce up the hotel or simply to be given as gifts.

Mist changed into a favorite nightshirt—soft blue flannel with a moon and star print—and picked four frames from the waiting supply. Setting them on a side table near the easel, she added two more. People seemed to like the winterberry scenes, and she might as well create extras while she had the correct paint on her palette.

Brush in hand, Mist set to work, first creating a backdrop of blue on each canvas and then carefully adding dark, slender branches with bright berries in varying tones of red. Each painting was slightly different, yet all followed the same pattern, an image Mist visualized in her mind. This year she'd taken to adding a touch of silver leaf to the winterberry paintings, just as she'd begun including gold leaf in a popular angel and cloud design. The paintings shimmered under the gallery lights and were an immediate hit with customers. The demand for her paintings had nearly doubled over the previous year, and that didn't even count larger custom orders, which had also become more frequent. She was pleased for Clive since word had spread that he had more than sapphires and jewelry to offer. She was pleased, too, for the customers and the paintings, because she felt each painting she created would find a way to the person who most needed it.

In general, Mist's subjects were sweet and light, often whimsical in nature. Winter paintings featured—aside from the winterberries and angels—such images as evergreen trees with pine cones, vintage sleighs, and old-fashioned toys peeking out of a wooden chest.

Spring and summer paintings tended to be brighter: a striped beach chair with the ocean in the background, a cluster of wildflowers tied with a purple ribbon, a sailboat under a ray of sunshine. Autumn brought fall colors into play: a trio of aspen trees in burnt orange and gold foliage, a cornucopia of fruit and nuts on a weathered tabletop.

Mist loved all the seasons, but her favorite was winter. Colder weather and snowy landscapes soothed her, and hot mulled cider warmed her heart as much as her body. In addition, the Christmas holidays afforded her a chance to work her own kind of magic on those around her, as well as on herself.

Time stood still, yet flew by, whenever Mist escaped into art. Finally, pleased with the six miniature pictures, she put up her paints and cleaned her brushes and left the finished pieces to dry. Quietly she tiptoed back down the hall, cautious to not wake Betty.

Maisie was just turning off the lights when Mist stepped into the kitchen. The smell of gingerbread filled the air, and twelve more sheets of siding for the house frame stood finished, the last batch of four just starting to cool.

"Thank you, Maisie," Mist said. Though spoken quietly, her words startled Maisie. This was a common reaction to Mist's unusual manner of walking softly. People rarely heard her approach.

"I was just heading out," Maisie said, flipping the lights back on. "But I did bake four extra sheets, plus you have the first four I put in, and the ones Betty made before that." She waved a mitten-clad hand in the direction of the cooling gingerbread.

"Wonderful," Mist said. "And the oven is still warm?"

Maisie nodded. "I turned it off a few minutes ago, after that last batch came out, but it's still warm."

"I think I'll do one more batch then," Mist said, setting the oven to the proper temperature again. "I want to go over tomorrow's arrivals anyway."

"Betty mentioned that all the guests are coming in on the same day, right? I hope they don't all show up at the same time." Maisie leaned against the kitchen doorway, fully bundled up in winter outerwear.

Mist walked over to Maisie and gently guided her to the front hallway. "Don't worry. Guests will arrive when they arrive, and Betty and I will be fine." She picked up the registration book and cradled it against her chest. "However, I will worry about you if you don't go home and get some rest. Both of you."

"Thanks," Maisie said, hugging Mist. "Call me if you need anything. I'll be at the shop all day." She pulled the faux-fur hood of her jacket up over her head and left.

Returning to the kitchen, Mist checked the preheated oven and slid four more trays of gingerbread in to bake. Making herself a cup of chamomile tea, she sat at the table and opened the registration book.

The room assignments hadn't been difficult this year. Since some of the guests had stayed at the hotel before, Mist was familiar with their preferences. Clara would want Room Sixteen, with its light, airy feel and view of the back courtyard. Her new gentleman friend would stay in the room next door, per Clara's firm instructions. Mist had prepared both of those rooms already, putting a favorite Christmas quilt in Clara's room, and an assortment of old train engines and cabooses in the other accommodation. Clara had mentioned her friend had a passion for model railroads. Mist paused to double check his name. Andrew.

Professor Nigel Hennessy had been a guest before, but only on his own. Now that he would have family with him, the small room he'd stayed in before wouldn't work. She'd assigned a suite of rooms that she'd used the year before for three sisters. This would allow the professor's family to be close yet have some space from each other.

Mist continued to examine the list of names and room assignments. The room with the extra alcove would be perfect for Greta and Rolf Weber, who were traveling with their two newly adopted children, Hanna and Jo. Mist noted the crossed-out e, a result of a second conversation with Greta Weber, which clarified that both children were girls. Jo was short for Josephine.

This left Michael Blanton's room, which was located right at the top of the stairs. He'd stayed in that room the year before and had requested it again. Mist felt a light flush creep up her neck as she remembered his most recent email. He'd indicated the same room would be smart, as he wouldn't disturb other guests if he stayed up late. He wouldn't need to pass their rooms and disrupt their sleep. Though Mist knew he often spent evenings in front of the fireplace, reading, she also hoped they'd have some time to visit. They'd grown closer over the past two Christmases. But, then again, Mist reminded herself, life had a way of changing unexpectedly. She couldn't predict the direction their friendship would take any more than she could predict a smooth flow of arrivals the following day.

Mist closed the book and returned it to the front desk. She checked the gingerbread sheets in the oven and, finding them ready, pulled them out and turned the oven off. Setting the coffee to brew in the morning, she turned out the kitchen lights and retired to her room. There was only one more thing to do at this point: get a decent night's rest to prepare for the busy day ahead.

FOUR

A wisp of sunlight filtered through the window of Mist's room as she exchanged her nightshirt for drawstring pants and a long-sleeved layer of lightweight fleece. It was nearly one in the morning before she went to bed, but she felt fresh and energetic. She wound her hair up on her head and wove a paintbrush through it to hold it in a bun, a trick a teacher had taught her, but with a pencil, instead.

Slipping her feet into ballet flats, she headed for the kitchen, where she flipped on both coffee makers—one would move to the front hallway at six thirty—and turned the oven on to preheat. Although Moonglow's breakfast customers would find a granola, fruit, yogurt, and pastry bar on the buffet, they would smell gingerbread throughout the meal. Clive would be there at seven o'clock to scramble eggs and potatoes for those looking for heavier fare. Mist smiled, thinking of how gallantly he'd offered to come over early to do this, when she knew full well he tiptoed into the front hallway at six thirty-one each morning for coffee anyway.

Three hours later, the townsfolk had eaten; breakfast clean-up was complete; and the last of four gingerbread sheets sat cooling on the counter. Mist turned her attention to the guest rooms.

Choosing items to individualize each room proved relatively easy. With Clara and Andrew's rooms already set, she moved on to the others. The Webers were first-timers, and the phone conversation when they made their reservation hadn't revealed anything personal beyond the recent adoption. She'd have to use her instincts to individualize the room. Ultimately, she decided on a basket of varied yarn skeins and knitting needles, which she placed unobtrusively on a cedar chest in a corner of their room. The collection of bright colors made the room brighter. Leaving a leather bag of marbles on a side table where she'd placed one of the unique doilies, she moved on to the next room.

When it came to the professor and his family, Mist had a bit more insight. The professor had visited two years before. He'd been cold and aloof until the end of his stay, when he softened and became quite friendly with the other guests. He had a favorite teacup, which she now placed on a tray with similar cups for his family, along with assorted PG Tips tea bags and packages of McVities Shortbread and Milk Chocolate Digestives. It would require only regular replenishment of hot water and biscuits to keep the professor and family warm and cozy when in their suite.

This left Michael Blanton's room, which posed no challenge at all. A main thread in their growing friendship was the love of reading. They'd had many discussions revolving around literature, and she'd gathered a substantial collection for his room's bookcase over the past few months. Their emails had swayed in the same direction over the past year, skirting more personal exchanges, a fact that had planted the notion in Mist's mind that perhaps she'd misinterpreted Michael's feelings toward her the previous Christmas.

Recalling a copy of Dickens' *A Tale of Two Cities* that Michael had been reading the first time she met him, she placed *Great Expectations* and *Oliver Twist* on the bookshelf, along with Faulkner's *Light in August*, Doctorow's *Ragtime*, Steinbeck's *East of Eden*, and Cather's *Death Comes for the Archbishop*. Although she knew he was a fan of classics, she added a few more recent favorites of her own: Jamie Ford's *The Hotel on the Corner of Bitter and Sweet*, Tracy Chevalier's *Girl with a Pearl Earring* and Sara Gruen's *Water for Elephants*. As a final touch, she filled a pottery tray with artsy bookmarks she'd found at a craft fair the past spring—some crafted of thin etched metal, some beaded and dangling, and some simply rice paper edged with gold ink.

Checking each accommodation a final time, Mist returned to her room, changed to a midcalf-length skirt of dark sage and a soft ivory tunic. She added a strand of mixed green aventurine and jasper beads, brushed her hair and secured it back with a brass barrette, and followed a commotion of shuffling and grunting to the front of the hotel, where she found Clive and Clayton busy in the main room, attaching the baked gingerbread to the plywood walls of the framed house.

Reminding the men not to worry if a few slabs broke in two, since decorations could cover any cracks, Mist moved on to the registration desk. She knew all the guests were scheduled to arrive that day but was unsure in what order. She sorted the registration cards first alphabetically but then rearranged them specifically to be in no order at all—not by name, not by anticipated timing, not by anything but an abstract scattering of the cards across the counter in a way that visually pleased her.

"Everything ready?" Betty asked, emerging from the kitchen. The fragrance of cinnamon followed her. "Ah," Betty added. "What a gracious outfit for greeting the guests. You always look beautiful in green."

Mist inhaled, exhaled, and smiled. "Thank you. Yes, everything is perfectly ready. I take it the hotel's traditional glazed cinnamon nuts are in the making. The guests will be pleased."

"Of course," Betty said. "It wouldn't be Christmas without a bowl of those nuts out here. They're just cooling now." She eyed the registration counter, silently choosing a location for the sweet treats.

"Even if just so the neighborhood children can sneak in and swipe some now and then?" Mist said. She and Betty both knew not all the candied treats would make it into guests' hands.

"Especially for that reason," Betty said. She grinned and returned to the kitchen.

Mist glanced over the registration cards again, set out a couple of pens, and checked on the progress in the main room. The front and sides of the gingerbread house were already covered. Clive and Clayton were starting on the back when Mist heard the front door open, and she turned to face the first incoming guests.

"Mist!" Clara Winslow rushed across the entryway and embraced Mist eagerly. "I've been so excited about this visit! I could hardly wait to get here. You look wonderful, as always. I feel calm and peaceful, just seeing you."

Mist returned Clara's embrace and smiled. "And seeing you makes me happy," Mist said.

"Let me introduce you," Clara said. She stepped back and took the hand of her companion, a slight, silver-haired gentleman of medium height. "This is Andrew."

"Glad to meet you, Andrew," Mist said as she shook his hand. "Welcome to the Timberton Hotel. We're so pleased you could join us this year."

"As am I," Andrew said. "Clara has spoken so highly of you all. I just had to come meet you myself."

"Don't let him fool you," Clara whispered to Mist. "He's just after the cookies from Betty's annual cookie exchange."

Andrew let out a warm, hearty laugh, and Mist instantly approved. "I admit the cookies were a draw, but that's not the only reason I'm here. I look forward to spending this lovely holiday with the equally lovely Clara." He beamed at Clara affectionately.

"Did I hear Clara Winslow's voice?" Betty emerged from the kitchen with a crystal bowl full of nuts, which she set on the front counter. She hugged Clara, shook hands with Andrew, and then hugged him too. "We're so happy to have you both here."

"Your rooms are ready," Mist said, motioning toward the registration desk. "Let me get you settled in. I'm sure you're tired from traveling."

"Indeed, Mist is right," Betty said. "We'll have plenty of time to visit. Let me help with your bags." She headed for the luggage, but Clive interrupted her.

"Oh, no you don't." When Clive stepped into the lobby, he was covered with crumbs of gingerbread and clumps of royal frosting. "I'll get those bags in a minute." He greeted Clara and Andrew enthusiastically from a short distance, then excused himself to wash the sweet, sticky building materials off his hands. As he left the room, the front door opened again.

"Professor Hennessy," Mist said, warmly welcoming the man who entered.

"Just Nigel this year, please," the professor said. Snow fell from a brimmed hat as he tipped it in greeting. "Please meet my sister, Chloe, and her daughter, Poppy."

"We're delighted to have you here for the holidays," Mist said.

"We are!" Betty said.

"I'm so glad you returned, Nigel. We missed you last year," Clara said. "This is my friend Andrew. He's a newcomer."

One of the best qualities of the Timberton Hotel's Christmas season was that many guests returned. This imbued the holiday with the atmosphere of a family reunion.

"We're busy!" Betty whispered to Clive as he returned to grab Clara and Andrew's bags.

"And getting busier," Clive said, nodding toward a window beside the doorway. Four more guests approached, carefully navigating the icy walkway.

"This will be the Weber party," Betty said to Mist. "Why don't I greet them while you show Professor Hennessy and his family to their suite?"

"That's an excellent idea," Mist said, realizing the entryway was quickly becoming crowded. Counting the current guests, herself, Betty, Clive and Clayton, who had joined in to help with luggage, nine people now occupied the foyer, and it was about to become thirteen. She and Betty had both hoped the guest arrivals would be spread out, but that was never entirely predictable in the hotel business. The wise move now would be to help the guests to their rooms so they could return downstairs to the larger front room once settled.

"Professor..." Mist turned to the Hennessy group. "May I show you all to your suite?"

"A spectacular idea," the professor said. He turned to his sister and niece. "What do you think, ladies?"

"Brilliant," Chloe said with a polite yet reserved smile.

Poppy nodded, stifling a yawn at the same time, which reminded Mist that international travel was lengthy and tiring.

"And remember to call me Nigel, my dear," the professor said kindly.

"I'll try," Mist said, but to her he would always be the professor.

Mist led the Hennessys to their suite and ushered them inside.

"It's lovely!" Chloe exclaimed, taking in the antique furnishings and elegant linens. "And the tea tray looks heavenly. I don't know if I've ever yearned for a cup of tea quite as much as I do this very minute."

"And she drinks a lot of tea," Poppy added. The first spoken words from the preteen brought a smile to Mist's face. The girl's voice was sweet and clear, almost angelic.

"You'll see you have two rooms, plus a sitting area," Mist said. "Relax and make yourselves at home. I'll bring up a pot of hot water in a few minutes."

She left the suite and took the back hallway to the kitchen, where she put a kettle of water on the stove to boil. Friendly chatter floated back from the front entryway as Betty and the Weber family finished up with greetings and registration. She could hear that Clive and Clayton had luggage delivery under control.

Mist poured herself a glass of cold water and sat down, taking advantage of the time it took the kettle to boil for tea. Betty had cleaned up after finishing the glazed nuts, and the kitchen sat ready for dinner preparation later on. She'd planned an easy meal anyway, knowing that guest arrivals would take priority. And, after all, Christmas Eve dinner, the holiday highlight at the Moonglow Café, was only two days away.

Mist caught the kettle before its sharp whistle could interfere with the greetings in the lobby. She poured a full pot and took it upstairs to the suite and then returned to the front entryway. Clive had just escorted the Weber family up the stairs, luggage in tow. Betty remained alone at the desk, putting the registration cards in order. Mist noted no more cards remained on the counter.

"We still have one more arrival, don't we?" Mist asked. She knew her casual tone didn't fool Betty, who was well aware how much Mist looked forward to seeing Michael Blanton.

"Actually, we don't," Betty said, quickly adding, "but don't worry. He's already here."

"He is?" Mist knew both her surprise and relief were evident. For a brief second, she'd thought Betty was going to say he had cancelled.

"Yes, he arrived right behind the Webers but asked to fill out the registration card later. I gave him the key to his room so he could rest."

Mist paused. "How did he seem?" she finally asked.

Betty remained quiet before answering. "Tired. He seemed tired but glad to be here." She reached over and rubbed Mist's hand in a motherly fashion. "Don't worry, Mist. He'll be down later, I'm sure. You'll find him in front of the fireplace."

"Reading in his favorite chair," Mist added. "Yes, I know you're right."

FIVE

The meal Mist served that evening was another simple one, this time deli sandwiches for dinner. The local residents who'd dined at the café the previous night didn't mind the casual cuisine. What they found was a collection of sandwich makings with just a few added features: fresh-baked artisan breads, seven types of mustards, an olive bar with a dozen Greek, Italian, and French varieties, and a massive dessert tray of miniature orange meringue tarts, chocolate-mint truffles, and petite squares of cinnamon-walnut baklava.

"Best deli I've ever been to," Clayton said, setting his loaded plate on a café table and sitting down, wide-eyed. Others at his table, mouths already full, nodded.

"Maisie, wouldn't it feel wonderful to sit down?" Mist said as she replenished bowls of Kalamata and Picholine olives. "Go enjoy a meal with your husband. Everything is under control." She nodded toward a stack of plates at the end of the buffet. Maisie, who had insisted on helping Mist set up the dinner offerings, didn't argue. She thanked Mist, selected a modest assortment of items from the buffet, and took a seat beside Clayton.

Mist retrieved a large pitcher of water from the beverage table and began to make the rounds, visiting with each table.

"A wonderful meal," Clara said as Mist topped off everyone's water glasses. Greta and Rolf Weber had joined Clara and Andrew for dinner. The four seemed to be hitting it off as if they'd known each other for years. Despite the age difference between the two couples—a good thirty years, Mist estimated—conversation flowed easily.

"I've read online reviews about the food here," Greta said. "Now I understand." A smile spread across Greta's round face, and the café lights glimmered in the woman's blue-gray eyes. Noticing the guest's tall, slender stature and whitish-blond hair, Mist felt certain she'd guessed Greta's heritage correctly: Swedish.

The professor, seated at a nearby table with his sister, joined the conversation. "Just you wait," he said. "The Christmas Eve meal here is exquisite. I'm planning to wear my best silk bow tie for the occasion."

"Outstanding," Rolf Weber said. "I love a good holiday meal, great food, great company. Don't you agree, girls?" He directed his question to a table some might call "the kids' table," though it wasn't so by official designation. The two Weber children had asked to sit with the professor's niece. Hanna and Poppy were both preteens; Jo was just a few years younger. The adults agreed without hesitation, glad to contain the children's banter to a different table, thus allowing themselves ample freedom of conversation.

Townsfolk spread around the room here and there. A few tables remained empty while others had an unoccupied seat or two.

Mist set a pitcher of raspberry lemonade in the center of the unofficial kids' table and looked around. There was still no sign of Michael Blanton, though it appeared the professor and Chloe had saved a place for him. Mist chided herself for feeling a twinge of disappointment. Surely he was just tired from his journey.

The buffet was dwindling, and Mist headed for the kitchen to restock the spread. Full platters created a more appetizing display, so she always prepared more food than needed. She could always do something with the leftovers. She usually stashed them in Room Seven's refrigerator, the room set aside for Timberton's unofficial homeless person, Hollister, who had become a frequent overnight visitor during the past year, as opposed to sporadic stays before. This pleased Mist immensely, as she'd tried hard to make the man feel welcome, to think of the hotel as his home, rather than the cubbyhole under the local railroad trestle, where he had lived for many years.

Several quick trips to the kitchen allowed Mist to reload the buffet for guests and townsfolk who had yet to arrive. As she topped off the olive bar, from the corner of her eye, she saw Michael stroll into the room quietly. Their eyes caught for a second as he sat in the chair the professor had saved for him. Mist headed back to the kitchen, pondering something she might have observed. Had he been limping when he came in? No, she told herself, she must have imagined it. If he'd had a relapse, surely he would have told her in one of his emails.

"Why don't you sit down and have something to eat?" Betty suggested. She and Clive were seated at the kitchen's center island, Clive on his second plateful of food, Betty enjoying a miniature tart.

"You both know I test everything as I prepare it," Mist said. "I suspect I often have a full meal before the food even leaves the kitchen."

Betty dabbed a bit of meringue off her lip with a napkin. "True. I've seen you do that."

"A job I would be happy to volunteer for," Clive said cheerfully before taking a bite of his sandwich.

"I'm sure you would." Mist laughed. "I may take you up on that sometime. That is, if you're not already in here swiping nibbles anyway."

"Which you often are," Betty said. She elbowed Clive teasingly and then turned back to Mist. "Go sit down and have a cup of tea and dessert then. I know there's an open seat at the professor's table."

"Not yet," Mist said with a slightly firmer tone than she intended. "It's the guests' first meal together. Let's let them enjoy it with each other. I'll spend time in the front parlor this evening while everyone gathers in front of the fireplace—or comes through to look at the tree, which is quite enchanting,"

Betty nodded and turned to Clive. "She's right. You found us a beauty this year."

"Why thank you, ladies," Clive said. "Don't mind if I say so myself: I agree."

Maisie poked her head into the kitchen as Betty and Clive left to bundle up for a chilly evening walk. "I'm going to clear plates, Mist. That way you can get started on preparations for the activities, if you want."

"Thank you, Maisie," Mist said. "I *will* feel better if I get started tonight, rather than tomorrow morning."

As Maisie headed back out to the café, Mist pulled dishes down from cupboards above the refrigerator, where she had stashed a marvelous find earlier that year from Secondhand Sally's: twelve large bowls of similar, yet varied, pottery designs. The glazes covered just about every color in the rainbow. From the first time she'd laid eyes on them, Mist knew exactly what she'd use them for. Now she set them around the center island, leaving one large, empty space in the middle.

"I have an idea," Mist said as Maisie brought an armful of dinner plates in from the café. "Is the professor's niece still out there? And maybe the Weber girls?"

"They certainly are, all three of them." Maisie laughed. "Giggling up a storm at that table of theirs. I'd say they've hit it off."

Mist smiled. "Perfect. Ask them if they'd like to help with a task in the kitchen."

"Are you up to what I think you are?" Maisie asked. "Should I tell them?"

"No, I wouldn't." Mist shook her head. "Let them be surprised. If they volunteer to help, they'll deserve a treat."

"Or several," Maisie qualified.

"Yes." Mist laughed. "Exactly."

A few minutes later, all three girls showed up in the kitchen. Whether their intention was simply to be polite or a genuine desire to help, their eyes lit up immediately as they watched Mist pile bag after bag and box after box of candy and other sweets on the table.

"Hello, Poppy," Mist said. "And how are you, Hanna and Jo?"

The three girls mumbled "hellos" and "fines," their eyes barely flickering away from the sugar-laden table.

"Okay then," Mist said. "I could certainly use your help. I just can't decide which bowls should hold which treats." She tilted her head slightly to the side, as if contemplating.

"I think we can handle this," Poppy said. The sisters nodded enthusiastically.

The girls set to work as Mist checked the front hallway, making sure there was plenty of coffee, as well as herbal tea for those who preferred to avoid caffeine in the evening. The dinner crowd in the cafe had thinned out, many heading home. A few people lingered, admiring old-fashioned ornaments on the Christmas tree.

Back in the kitchen, Mist was not surprised to find the three girls thoroughly enjoying their work. An animated discussion was in progress, regarding whether candy canes would look better in a green pottery bowl—too traditional, one girl argued—or a bluish bowl that was close to turquoise in color. Turquoise won out for the candy canes as the third girl, while the discussion continued, filled the green bowl with gumdrops. In the end, contrast appeared to win out over matching colors. Licorice strings filled a brown bowl, ribbon candy practically spilled over the edges of a red bowl, and round peppermint candies topped off a yellow bowl. Other bowls held miniature star-shaped cookies, chocolate wafers, cinnamon candies, and lemon drops. Naturally, for Betty's sake, a purple bowl held caramels. Vermont maple sugar, crystallized ginger, malted milk balls, butter mints, coconut bonbons, and saltwater taffy overflowed other containers.

"So what do you think?" Mist asked, looking over the finished display.

"Brilliant," Poppy said.

"Rad," Jo quipped.

"Nobody says 'rad,'" Hanna said. "But it does look amazing."

Mist nodded, her expression pensive, yet her eyes sparking with mischief. "Yes, I agree. But... what do you think of the variety... a good combination of tastes?"

The girls looked at each other and then back at Mist.

"I think it would help if you each tested a few of the decorations," Mist said. "Not *all* of you test *all* of them, mind you," she cautioned. A hotel full of sick preteens would put a damper on the holiday spirit.

"We can take turns choosing," Poppy suggested.

"An excellent idea," Mist agreed. "Who will start?"

"*You* start," Hanna said to Mist, surprising them all.

"All right," Mist said, considering the options. She finally settled on a small piece of crystallized ginger, not unlike something she might find in trail mix. Nodding in approval, she left the girls to complete their task, instructing them to cover each bowl with the plastic wrap she pulled out of a drawer when done. That settled, she retired to her room, brushed her hair, washed her face, and headed to the front parlor to visit with guests.

SIX

"Why, Queen Elizabeth, of course." The professor announced this proudly as Mist walked into the front parlor. Mist felt a momentary impulse to look over her shoulder in case the Queen herself was entering the room behind her. Instead, she quickly caught onto the discussion in progress.

"Exactly," Michael said. "I was quite sure you would know that." Dressed in khaki pants and a soft brown sweater, he sat in front of the fireplace, a closed book in his lap. Mist recognized it from the binding: Faulkner's *Light in August*.

"Please don't get up," Mist said as the professor started to stand. "I just came to say hello and to see if anyone needs coffee or tea or perhaps a bowl of Betty's cinnamon-glazed nuts."

"Not at all necessary, my dear," the professor said.

"I agree," Michael said. "Sit with us, instead." Mist was quite sure she saw a twinkle in his eye as he patted the seat of the chair closest to him.

"I'll do that," she agreed, sitting down. "So, what's this talk of Queen Elizabeth? Are you discussing the annual Queen's speech that you listen to each year in England on Christmas?"

"As a matter of fact, we're talking about gingerbread," Michael said. "Something in this room seemed to bring up the topic." He smiled.

"I can't imagine what that could be." Mist's attempt to look clueless failed, and she laughed at herself. She looked over her shoulder, toward the corner of the room. Clive and Clayton had done a magnificent job of finishing the basic gingerbread house. Once the decorations were added, it would be stunning—unless the girls ate them all, of course. She smiled at the thought, knowing it wasn't likely.

"Queen Elizabeth I is credited with inventing the first gingerbread man," the professor explained. "It is said she had them made in the likeness of foreign dignitaries to present to them when they came to visit."

"How interesting," Mist said. "If I had thought of that, I could have done the same thing for arriving guests. Not a bad idea," she mused. "A tray of Michael and Nigel cookies."

"And what about me?" Clara said, entering the room.

"Certainly, Clara," the professor said. "We could have Clara cookies too. Even Mist cookies—why not?"

"Those would be especially sweet, I think," Michael said, barely loud enough for Mist to hear, though Clara smiled.

"So, catch me up on this silly conversation," Clara said. "Are you saying Queen Elizabeth invented gingerbread cookies?"

The professor shook his head. "No, that is entirely incorrect."

Mist smiled. Few people could get away with the professor's tone and speech without it sounding offensive. Yet, from him, it was charming.

"Gingerbread biscuits," the professor continued, "go back centuries. That would be cookies to those of you on this side of the pond, I suppose. In any case, they were traded and sold at medieval festivals, and by monasteries and pharmacies. Gingerbread has a long history of medicinal uses. Even the Egyptians used it for ceremonial purposes."

"But Queen Elizabeth I made the gingerbread man popular?" Clara asked.

Michael stepped in this time. "It was really after *St. Nicholas Magazine*, a children's publication, published 'The Gingerbread Boy' in 1875 that the cookies became part of general culture, associated with Christmas, in particular."

"Ah, yes," the professor said. "One of a whole realm of tales called 'Fleeing Pancake' stories. They usually involve some type of baked good that runs away, is chased by a variety of people or animals, and is eventually eaten."

"Rather tragic, I'd say," Clara commented.

"I agree," Michael said. "Yet that's the nature of much literature. Look at *Hansel and Gretel*, for example, since we're talking about gingerbread already."

"True," the professor said. "The Brothers Grimm tales are hardly known for lighthearted plots. In *Hansel and Gretel,* the children fare well in the end but start out, quite sadly, abandoned by their parents. And they only attain their ultimate salvation by throwing a witch in the oven."

All four glanced at the yet undecorated gingerbread house and then turned back toward each other.

"So that gave us the gingerbread house that is so popular today?" Clara asked.

"Yes and no," Michael said. "Some food historians say gingerbread houses were around before *Hansel and Gretel* was published."

"Which was in 1812," the professor noted.

"Yes. And that story is really what made them popular," Michael continued. "German bakeries started selling them already decorated. And they became especially popular around Christmas."

"*Lebkuchen,*" Rolf Weber said, tossing the German word for gingerbread into the conversation as he entered the room. "That was always a special treat when I was a child, growing up in Nuremberg. Sometimes bread, other times cookies. We had some marvelous molded shapes as well. Those carved molds are very collectible these days."

"Indeed," the professor said. "I've seen them in gingerbread museums."

"Gingerbread museums, really?" Clara asked.

"Absolutely. The Muzeum Piernicka, for example, has a splendid collection. If you're ever in Torun, Poland, you should go." The professor looked quite pleased with himself for offering this suggestion. "Visitors can take tours and participate in making gingerbread."

"That would be fascinating," Mist said.

Rolf took a seat, joining the others. "If you really want to experience *Lebkuchen* at its best, you must go the *Christkindlesmarkt* in Nuremberg. It is worth a December trip to Germany just to breathe in the smells at the market. Isn't that right, dear?" He motioned to Greta, who had just finished pouring a cup of coffee in the entryway and came into the front parlor to join her husband and the others.

"Oh, yes," Greta said. "We went every year before moving to the United States."

"So you are both from Germany," Clara said. "How wonderful."

Greta shook her head. "I was born and raised in Sweden but went to college in Germany, which is where I met Rolf. But we have gingerbread traditions in Sweden too. My mother always made *pepparkakor*, a very thin ginger cookie. We have a tradition. You place a *pepparkakor* in the palm of your hand, make a wish, and then tap the middle with your index finger." Greta set her coffee down and demonstrated with an invisible cookie. "If it breaks into three pieces, your wish will come true."

"A lovely idea," Mist said. "I'm sure we all have wishes tucked away somewhere inside us, especially around the holidays."

"I know I do," Greta said. "I would wish for Hanna and Jo to feel more comfortable in our home. It's still so new to them, even though they've lived with us for over a year, since they lost their parents in a terrible accident."

"I'm so sorry," Mist said. The others echoed her words, and Greta and Rolf accepted them appreciatively.

"We only officially adopted the girls two months ago," Greta continued. "Hanna often dreams of her old home. Jo's good about comforting her, which is sweet, especially considering she's nine and Hanna is twelve. I suspect they would wish for their former lives back, though they're not unhappy with us. Being together is a comfort to them. They've been laughing and playing more since the adoption was finalized and they know we are a permanent family."

"How about you, Clara?" Rolf asked, noticing Clara wringing her hands momentarily.

Clara glanced toward the entryway and back at the group. "Andrew is resting upstairs, but I can talk about this. We've been discussing consolidating our houses—giving up one and keeping the other, together. It's not easy making the decision. We're each fond of our own homes. They hold a lot of history. I wish that we can come to a decision that feels right for both of us. I know he wishes for the same thing."

"I would be quite chuffed to get settled into a new home myself," the professor said. "This is a big transition, moving to a new country—exciting but unsettling." He looked over at Michael. "And I can guess what Michael would wish for: more time to read."

"And perhaps more time to visit Timberton," Clara said, smiling.

"I'll go along with those," Michael said.

"All wonderful wishes," Mist said. She stood. "It's time for me to get back to the kitchen. I need to start preparing for tomorrow's breakfast."

"What would you wish for, Mist?" Michael asked as Mist started to walk away. "A larger dining room for the café? More time to paint?"

Mist turned and smiled. "Well, I would wish for peoples' wishes to come true. And for you all to have a lovely night."

SEVEN

Strawberry-rhubarb muffins, sliced honeydew melon, and a chafing dish of herbed frittata graced the buffet the following morning, along with granola, blueberry yogurt, fresh-squeezed orange juice, and coffee. The simple morning meal—at least simple by Mist's standards—allowed her to spend more energy on the many other tasks of the day. Clive and Clayton would complete the back side of the roof for the undecorated gingerbread house. Mist would cater to guest needs, and Betty would prepare for her favorite holiday event: the annual cookie exchange, scheduled for that afternoon.

With the additional activity surrounding the gingerbread house, Betty had, for the first time, opted out of baking cookies herself. Although she loved baking Christmas cookies, there was just too much going on, especially with the kitchen fully committed to gingerbread for several days in a row. Even in the off moments when the oven wasn't churning out sweet slabs of molasses-laced siding, Mist had needed it for meal prep, though the café offerings had been kept simple on purpose.

"I'm here to help," Maisie said as she stepped in through the kitchen's side door. She took off her jacket, hung it on a wall hook, and deposited a knit cap and gloves on the counter.

"You didn't need to come over," Mist said, kitchen towel in hand. She was grateful for the extra help but aware Maisie had guests at home.

"Oh yes I did." Maisie laughed as she took the towel from Mist and began drying the last of the breakfast dishes. "Clayton's parents are driving me crazy with 'first grandchild' chatter. I can't even imagine what they'll be like next year with 'baby's first Christmas.' I had to get out of the house. The hotel is calmer than our house right now. Speaking of which, where is everyone?"

Mist smiled. The time right after breakfast was often the most peaceful part of the day, as guests headed off with varying plans. "Betty went to the gallery to deliver an order of paintings. Clara, Andrew, Greta, and Rolf went out for a drive to see the winter scenery. The girls are down at the town plaza, building a snow maiden—their version of a snowman, they said. And Michael and the professor are in the front parlor, extremely focused on a game of chess, though they're also continuing a discussion of nineteenth-century Russian literature—Dostoyevsky was the last author mentioned, I believe."

"Any idea how many people are participating in the cookie exchange?" Maisie asked.

"I'd say fifteen to twenty," Mist said. "All the regulars, plus a few new residents of Timberton. Betty made sure to let them know they were welcome."

Maisie nodded, placed the last dried dish in a cupboard, and set the towel aside. "Well, I know Millie will be here. She stopped by the shop the other day to pick up a holly wreath and said she'd be bringing gingersnaps—a special recipe from her grandmother.

"I'm not surprised," Mist said. "I suspect we'll have more ginger-related treats than other years. The gingerbread house seems to have inspired that theme."

"Don't worry," Maisie said. "There'll be all types of cookies. I heard Sally is bringing at least one variety of french *macarons*, Marge made 'Kitchen Sink Cookies' and Glenda's contributing vegan sugar cookies."

"We have *kourabiedes* coming from Kristiana too," Mist said.

"Do I know Kristiana?" Maisie tipped her head to the side, trying to match the name with a person. "And what are *kourabiedes*?"

"Kristiana is the new baker," Mist said. "She just moved here a few weeks ago from Greece. She said Sparta, but I don't remember the name of her town. *Kourabiedes* are traditional little Christmas cakes with a healthy dose of cloves."

"The church guild ladies are bringing several batches of cookies but didn't say what kind," Maisie said. She left to check the café and returned to the kitchen. "Should I start setting everything up, maybe put out paper plates now, for people to fill with cookie assortments?"

"We're using baskets this year," Mist said, smiling.

"Baskets?" Maisie asked as Betty entered the room, back from the gallery.

"Yes," Betty said, jumping into the conversation. "Mist found some light balsa wood baskets, like berry baskets, but a little bigger. They're just the right size to hold a couple dozen cookies. I loved the idea of sending people home with something they can reuse. Mist even decorated them with her usual artistic flair."

"I simply painted a holly leaf on one side of each basket," Mist said. "We'll have clear cellophane and red organza ribbon so they can be wrapped as gifts."

"That's a wonderful idea," Maisie said. "Even though I bet most people plan to take them home to enjoy themselves, or with their families."

"Even better," Mist said. "Sometimes a gift to oneself is the best kind. We all deserve something special now and then."

"I agree." Mist turned to see Michael leaning in the door to the front hallway. Something about his casual stance caused Mist to blush. Yet the same casual way he leaned against the doorjamb reminded her she had yet to see him walk across a room. Had she or had she not noticed a limp when he first took his seat in the café?

"Chess game over?" Mist asked. "Or just taking a break between Tolstoy and Chekhov?"

"Nigel went down to the town plaza to see how the girls were doing," Michael said.

"Busy, I imagine," Maisie said. "They stopped by the shop on the way down there and picked up some flowers and greenery that I had that was still pretty but not fresh enough to sell. They want to put a wreath of flowers on the snow maiden's head when they finish and a few on her skirt, as well."

"Her skirt?" Betty looked puzzled.

"They'll pack extra snow around the base of the figure," Maisie offered as further explanation. "At least that's how they explained it."

"A skirt of snow? How clever," Mist said. "And a beautiful idea to decorate it with flowers too." She envisioned a watercolor version of the idea.

"If you get a break, we could walk down and see how it's turning out." Michael looked directly at Mist as he made the suggestion.

"An excellent idea," Betty said. "There's no need for you to work all day. You know how I love playing hostess for the cookie exchange. And Maisie can help me here."

"Absolutely," Maisie said. "Just tell me where the baskets are, and I'll set everything up."

"I suppose a short break would be nice," Mist said. She glanced out the kitchen window and saw that snow flurries were dancing across the winter landscape.

"Yes, it would indeed," Betty said. "Go bundle up. Maisie can help me set up. I know where everything is."

Encouraged by the others, as well as drawn by the idea of spending some time with Michael, Mist retreated to her room. She emerged wearing a patchwork cape of heavy fabric, the hood resting delicately on her head. With a heavy sweater underneath and worn knitted mittens on her hands, she would be warm enough for the short excursion.

"Go," Betty urged. "We'll be fine."

* * *

Snow gathered on Mist's hooded cape as she and Michael walked toward the town plaza. Side by side, each took turns glancing at the other while focusing most of their attention on the sidewalk ahead.

"You look beautiful, Mist," Michael said. "Like a woodland apparition who has appeared magically in a snowy glen. The cape suits you—unique and mystical."

Mist laughed. "Just scraps from the thrift store's fabric bin."

"That you used to create a piece of art," Michael clarified. "Not a surprise, of course. Everything you touch becomes magical in some way." Whether to catch a bit of the magic or to prompt even more, he reached out and took Mist's mitten-clad hand in his own.

Mist squeezed Michael's hand, accepting the gesture of closeness. "You're limping," she said quietly. She'd noticed as soon as they'd left the kitchen, before they even reached the front door.

"Yes," Michael said, adding nothing more.

They walked in silence for a moment, the simple statement and confirmation hanging in the air.

"This is why you weren't able to make the trip here in the spring," Mist finally said. It wasn't a question.

She already understood and wasn't going to push for an explanation. She hadn't asked for one earlier in the year either, when he'd changed his travel plans and indicated he'd be back at Christmas, as always.

"Yes," Michael repeated. "It was an unexpected recurrence." He stopped and turned Mist toward him. "I didn't want to worry you. It was just a small tumor, and it hadn't spread. The doctors feel they got it all."

"Again," Mist said.

"Yes, again." Michael pulled Mist closer and wrapped his arms around her, holding her. They stood without moving for several minutes.

"Life is mysterious," Mist whispered. "We never know what the future has in store, not even an hour ahead."

"Well, I say we try to take that next hour and make it whatever we want." Michael stepped back, tilted his head to one side, and looked at Mist, seeking a co-conspirator to test fate.

Mist nodded. "I accept the challenge," she said in a most serious tone. "I propose lingering in the town plaza with a snow maiden, followed by enjoying hot mulled cider in front of the hotel's fireplace."

"I agree with your plan completely," Michael said, "with one exception."

"And what would that be?" Mist searched his face, noted, as she had many times before, the remarkable gray-green-copper color of his eyes.

"Well, if we're tempting fate for only one hour, I believe we should make that hour exceptional." Michael smiled.

Mist noted a bit of mischief in his expression. "A snow maiden and hot mulled cider won't make for an exceptional hour?"

"Almost, but not quite." Michael leaned closer, his lips inches from Mist's. "Don't you agree?" As Mist smiled, he kissed her softly. "Now it's exceptional."

"Yes," Mist said. "Exceptional indeed."

EIGHT

Animated chatter flowed from the interior of the hotel as Mist and Michael stepped through the front door. The exceptional hour had stretched into three, combining snow maiden play with a visit to Clive's gallery, another to Marge's candy store, and a long walk through the wintery Timberton scenery.

As Michael took his favorite spot beside the fireplace, Mist went to retrieve the promised hot mulled cider. She passed through the café, now busy with Betty's cookie exchange in full swing. Holiday spirit decked the air as townsfolk filled their baskets with assorted treats. Maisie stood by with cellophane and ribbon and discussed recipes with cheerful participants.

Leaving the cookie enthusiasts to enjoy themselves, Mist heated up the cider and filled a pot with the hot beverage. She delivered it to the front entryway, where mugs already waited at the coffee and tea service area.

Clara, Andrew, Greta, and Rolf had returned from their drive and now sat with Michael in the front parlor. They were in the middle of a discussion, which continued as Mist poured mugs of cider and carried them into the room.

"You do have a lovely garden," Clara said to Andrew. "I can see why you would hate to give that up. The rhododendrons alone are magnificent. Plus you have the outdoor deck."

"I know you're fond of the landscaping at my place," Andrew said. "But the kitchen in your house is wonderful. It's much more modern than mine, and more spacious."

"Is this a garden versus kitchen discussion?" Mist asked as she handed a mug of cider to Greta and a second mug to Clara. "Both sound lovely."

"We're still debating which house to give up and which to keep since we're combining households," Clara said.

The professor and Chloe entered the room. "I have an easy answer," the professor said. "Just send one of the houses here. I need to find a place to live before the semester begins." He turned down an offer of cider in favor of tea.

"Or just a flat, Nigel," Chloe said. "While you look around. No need to rush into a purchase before you find a place that feels right."

"Yes, a flat, that could work," the professor agreed. "Carry on then." He took a sip of tea and settled back in a chair, looking professorial indeed in his argyle sweater-vest and wire-rimmed glasses.

Greta sighed. "I'm glad we're not house hunting. We're planning to remodel, though, to add an extra bedroom. Right now Hanna and Jo are sharing a room."

"They don't seem to mind," Rolf said.

"True," Greta said. "We hear quite a bit of serious talking late at night."

"And giggling after a little while," Rolf added.

"Perhaps sharing is nice for them right now," Mist said, leaving unspoken the fact they were going through dramatic life adjustments. It was not her place to share personal situations, but she knew Greta and Rolf would understand the thought behind her statement. "They seem to enjoy each other's company," she added.

"Yes." Rolf nodded his head. "I think you're right, Mist. They don't seem to suffer from any sibling conflicts and stay very close to each other. Sharing a room may be all right, at least until we can finish the remodel."

The front door opened and closed, and Clive's voice boomed out, "What? No Christmas music to go with this holiday scene?"

"An excellent idea," Betty said. She passed by him with a basket brimming with cookies, which she placed on a coffee table near the visiting guests. "And I'm sure your sudden visit has everything to do with music and nothing to do with the cookie exchange in progress, right?" Her smirk, combined with the obvious way Clive's eyes followed the path of the cookies, made everyone laugh.

"Music is a wonderful idea," Mist said. "I have just the right selection." She stood and walked to a closet that housed the hotel's sound system. Strains of traditional Christmas instrumentals began to flow from overhead speakers.

"Help yourselves," Betty said, gesturing to the basket of baked treats. "We have plenty to go around."

"Don't mind if I do," Clive said. "But here, I don't want to be greedy." He held the basket out to each guest before taking a cookie himself.

Betty returned to the café to help Maisie wrap the cookie baskets. Mist followed, leaving the guests to enjoy their cider, cookies, and music together.

With the last of the cookie baskets wrapped and townsfolk headed home with their cellophane bundles, Betty and Mist sat at the kitchen's center island.

"Quite a busy day," Betty said. She leaned forward and folded her arms on the countertop.

"Why don't you take a break, maybe a short nap?" Mist suggested. As gracious a hostess as Betty had been for the cookie exchange, full of smiles and compliments, Mist now noticed how tired she seemed.

"I hate to leave you with all the work," Betty said, though clearly tempted by the idea. "I'm sure there's more I could help you with now."

Mist stretched both arms over her head and then lowered them to rest in her lap. "There's very little work to do, Betty. Maisie is doing a great job cleaning up the café. I'm serving a simple dinner later, and the guests are content in the front parlor, enjoying each other's company. Besides, I took a three-hour break earlier, remember?" She patted Betty's hand in a matronly way that seemed to reverse their roles, if not their ages. "Take some time to read a book or just rest. You can help later with the pomanders."

"Oh, yes." Betty's face brightened. "I forgot we were going to do that with the guests this evening.

Fine, I'll rest a bit now and help with the pomanders later. I can almost smell the scent of oranges and cloves, just thinking about it."

Mist smiled as she watched Betty head out of the kitchen. The idea of having the guests decorate oranges with whole cloves this year had really been Betty's, a result of a morning conversation a few weeks before while Betty, Maisie, and Mist had been cleaning up from breakfast. A cheerful discussion of childhood holiday memories had evolved into possible activities for guests. All three had agreed that the pomanders would be a great idea.

"You actually convinced Betty to rest?" Maisie said as she entered the kitchen. She set the leftover cellophane and ribbon on a counter and sat down across from Mist. "How did you manage that?"

"I reminded her of the pomanders," Mist said. "Because she had something to look forward to, she no longer needed to worry about something now."

Maisie nodded. "Clever, and a reminder that I need to bring you those supplies. I have everything ready, including a few sharp utensils to poke holes in the oranges for the cloves, and ribbons in white, gold, and silver. I brought extra ribbon, too, like you requested."

"Wonderful," Mist said. "The finished pomanders can either hang from hooks or rest in the tub over there." She gestured to a large copper container she had used for a flower arrangement the previous year.

"That will be perfect," Maisie said, standing back up. "I'll drop everything off later this afternoon.

Clayton's mom is cooking tonight, so we won't be here for dinner."

"It'll be a small crowd tonight—hotel guests, plus a few regulars," Mist said.

"You know they're just saving up their appetites for your Christmas Eve dinner tomorrow night." Maisie said. "What are you serving this year anyway?"

"I have a printed list this year," Mist said.

"A list?" Maisie laughed. "Dare I ask if it's an actual menu?"

Mist smiled. "You know I don't believe in menus."

"I know you don't," Maisie said. "You run the most amazingly successful café without ever putting a word on paper."

"These words are simply decorations." Mist crossed the room and pulled a sheet of rice paper from a folder and set it on the center countertop. Maisie's eyes widened as she looked over the masterpiece of calligraphy and watercolors.

Christmas Eve Dinner at the Moonglow Café

Rosemary-Orange Roasted Chicken
Cherry-Balsamic Pork Loin
Pomegranate, Pecan, and Brie Salad
Honey-Roasted Butternut Squash with
Cranberries and Feta
Sautéed Mushrooms in a Browned Butter,
Garlic and Thyme Sauce
Cheddar Chive Biscuits
Chocolate-Caramel Tart

"This is exquisite!" Maisie exclaimed. "Not to mention deliciously appetizing. Are you going to post this somewhere near the entry? Or did you have them printed for each table?"

Mist retrieved the folder and opened it, removing additional sheets, each one handwritten, individual, and artfully decorated.

"Of course." Maisie smiled. "I should have guessed they'd all be originals."

"There is one for each guest room," Mist said. "I'll use the extra ribbon you brought to tie them after I roll each one like a scroll, and then I'll place them in each room tomorrow afternoon with a small fruit and cheese plate."

"I wouldn't mind being a guest here," Maisie sighed.

Mist set the non-menu down and hugged Maisie. "You are welcome anytime, Maisie. Everyone is welcome here, always."

NINE

"I'm making a heart," Poppy said as she pressed a whole clove into her orange. She sat on the floor in the front parlor in her faded jeans and a red sweater with the words BAH, HUMBUG stenciled on the front. The Weber girls sat beside her, each working on a variation of pomander style. Hanna's orange already had the start of a zigzag pattern that ran horizontally. Jo had chosen to wrap ribbons around hers first and now was adding cloves in a haphazard fashion, as if they were afterthoughts.

The atmosphere in the room contradicted the words on Poppy's sweater as Burl Ives sang to everyone to have a "holly, jolly Christmas." Clara and Andrew laughed together on the sofa as Rolf, elbow propped on the fireplace mantel, told family-friendly jokes. Greta and Chloe admired the hotel's Christmas tree, which was lavishly decked out with garlands and twinkling lights. Betty stood beside them, telling stories about each of the old-fashioned ornaments— some passed down through the years, others made recently by local schoolchildren. The professor, predictably, sat with Michael, the two men engrossed in a literary discussion regarding Charles Dickens' motivation in writing *A Christmas Carol*, noting the author's concern with the spiraling effects of poverty on children following a visit to a London school.

Mist watched the scene from the arched entryway, delighted to see not only how spirited and happy the gathering was but also the way the guests interacted with each other. Newcomers, as well as those who'd spent many holiday seasons in Timberton before, blended as if they'd known each other for years. Mist liked to think of it as more than just the right combination of décor, food, music, and activities; she envisioned a thread of magic weaving through the small crowd, turning strangers into friends and friends into family.

"You're dangerously close to the mistletoe, you know," a voice whispered.

Mist turned to find Michael had managed to sneak up beside her while she was watching Poppy hold up her finished pomander, the heart design accentuated by gold ribbons. Mist looked up at the traditional cluster of leaves and berries hanging almost directly above and stepped back to examine it, as if just at that moment realizing Maisie had ordered the mistletoe, and Clive had securely fastened it in the archway. "And now I'm not," she said, a sly smile spreading across her face. She ducked away toward the kitchen as he reached for her, leaving him shaking his head at her impish behavior.

"Playing hard to get?" Betty asked as Mist took a seat at the kitchen's center island.

"I thought you were sharing ornament history by the Christmas tree," Mist said, surprised to find her friend had also left the front parlor.

"I just took a break to refill the bowl with the glazed cinnamon nuts," Betty said. "But you're dodging the question, aren't you? Hmm?"

Mist sighed. "I'm not playing hard to get. At least I don't think so." She propped both elbows on the counter and then her chin on her hands, silver bangles chiming softly as she moved her arms.

"I'm teasing you, Mist," Betty said. "You're not the type of person to play games. But I sense you're hesitant. You and Michael have had a connection from the start."

"You're right," Mist said. "I've always felt close to him, from the first time I met him three years ago. He's intelligent and gentle, perceptive about the world, and reserved but not standoffish."

"Sounds very much like someone else I know," Betty said, reaching across the table to touch Mist's hand. "Someone special to all of us here in Timberton but who also deserves to have her own life."

Mist stood to fix a cup of tea for herself and a mug of coffee for Betty and sat back down, setting both hot beverages on the table. "This is my life, Betty: the hotel, the café, you, Clive, everyone here in Timberton."

"And Michael?" Betty asked. She sipped her coffee and waited.

Mist opened her arms wide, as if including not only the kitchen but the entire world in her answer. "Michael is part of life here, just as everyone is who comes and goes from Timberton. And we are a part of their lives as well. Life does not exist solely on a physical plane. Our lives are interwoven as soon as we cross paths."

Clive, who had just entered the room while Mist was speaking, raised his eyebrows, turned, and tiptoed out. Both Betty and Mist laughed at Clive's reaction to Mist's unique worldview.

"Don't worry, Betty," Mist said. "We are all exactly where we are meant to be."

"For now," Betty added.

"Yes, for now," Mist said. "After all, 'now' is the only time there ever is."

TEN

Sunshine flowed through the window and between the branches of the Christmas tree, casting cheerful ribbons of light around the front parlor. Poppy, Hanna, and Jo carried bowl after bowl of sweets in from the kitchen, placing them on a long folding table that had been set up to hold the edible decorations for the gingerbread house. Licorice, gumdrops, and candy canes all vied for attention, as if shouting, "Me first, me first!"

Greta and Rolf relaxed on the sofa, smiling as they watched the three girls arrange the bowls. Michael sat in his usual chair beside the fireplace, also observing, while the professor and Chloe examined the ornaments on the tree. Clara and Andrew were expected back soon from a post-breakfast walk.

"This activity is not just for the girls," Mist said, her statement as close to an order as her sly smile could manage. She stood in the archway, dressed casually in a burgundy smocked dress that hit midcalf, just above her work boots, long sleeves rolled up, ready for an afternoon in the kitchen. Although the gingerbread house decorating was meant only for hotel guests, the Christmas Eve meal that evening would draw a crowd from the town as well.

"We don't want to take away from the girls' fun," Chloe said, turning from the tree. "It's so nice to see them enjoying themselves."

"Indeed," the professor agreed.

"And I'm glad to see Poppy making friends easily," Chloe added.

"I'm happy the girls are working together too," Mist said. "However…" She paused, eyeing the adults in the room. "With a gingerbread house this size, we could use everyone's help."

"You're even allowed to sample the goods as you decide where to begin," Betty added, as she stepped into the room to add one more bowl of candy to the table.

Rolf laughed and stood up. "Well, in that case, I'd better volunteer my time and effort." He strolled over to the table and tested a chocolate mint, then a second.

"For the greater good, of course," Greta said teasingly.

"Exactly," Rolf said after swallowing and patting his belly.

The professor cleared his throat and joined Rolf. "Well, I'd jolly well better help out," he said as he surveyed the table of sweets. He reached for the bowl of gumdrops, reconsidered, then picked out a cinnamon candy and popped it into his mouth. "Ah, quite a blast to the taste buds!" he announced.

One by one, the adults joined in. They discussed dividing up the work: the girls started in on the front door and windows; Michael applied frosting along corners; Greta and Rolf tackled one side of the rooftop; and Clara and Andrew returned from their walk to tackle the other. Hours passed as the group slowly adorned the structure one sweet piece at a time. After all was said and done, they stood back and viewed their masterpiece.

"It's exquisite!" Clara exclaimed. "And big enough to step inside, provided you duck through the doorway. I've never seen anything like it!"

Rolf nodded while swinging a red licorice string like a lasso. "I must say I agree." He turned to Poppy and Hanna, who stood nearby. "How clever of you girls to use pairs of candy canes to create hearts alongside each window."

"Thanks," Hanna said. The girls exchanged high fives.

"And look at that wreath above the door," Greta said. "Where did you get the flat green leaf shapes? And that cinnamon candy scattered on top looks just like berries. Very clever and creative of you."

"Betty brought those out," Poppy said. "They're candy lime fruit slices. We layered them on top of each other in a circle."

"Except for all the ones Jo ate," Hanna pointed out.

"Hey, I only ate a couple!" Jo said, sticking her head out of the doorway. Crouched on her hands and knees, she looked even younger than her nine years. "Well, maybe I ate more than a couple... like four." She paused as her older sister crossed her arms. "Or five. But you both ate all those milk chocolate raspberry creams."

Greta and Chloe exchanged looks. "I hope we don't have a stomachache coming on in the near future," Greta said.

"Never fun," Chloe sympathized. "Especially on holiday."

The front door opened, and Clive and Clayton entered. Clive whistled at the sight of the decorated house. Clayton slapped Clive on the back. "Not bad, Clive. It hasn't fallen down yet." Both men laughed.

Jo, unsettled by the suggestion that the structure above her might come crashing down, scuttled out. Poppy and Hanna, not at all worried, crouched down one at a time and disappeared inside.

"It's a good thing we made that doorway three feet high and almost two feet across," Clayton said.

Clive nodded. "Yep, you're right. I never even thought about the inside. Just seemed it would look better with a big entrance."

"You know…," Mist whispered as she walked past both men toward the kitchen, "it's what's inside a house that really matters."

"I suppose so," Clive said, nodding.

Clayton agreed. "Speaking of which, I have a house full of family. I'd better get back there before my mother and Maisie decide to remodel or something equally traumatic."

"Putting out fires before they start, good idea," Clive said.

Laughing, Clayton headed out. Soon the others disbursed to rest in their rooms before the large evening meal or bundled up to enjoy the lightly falling snow outdoors. Michael and the professor started a new game of chess, Clive went outside to bring in firewood for the evening, and Jo joined the two older girls inside what was now certainly the sweetest building in all of Timberton.

* * *

"What can I do to help?" Betty said. She sat at the kitchen's center island watching Mist cut butternut squash into one-inch squares. A bowl of already sliced mushrooms rested on the table nearby. The scents of mixed herbs and spices drifted through the air from main courses roasting in the oven.

"You are helping already," Mist said.

"How is that?" Betty's smile was both kind and resigned. Mist's subtle techniques for refusing help were nothing new. In truth, she knew Mist felt more comfortable doing the work herself, though she always welcomed company.

"You are inspiring me with your presence," Mist said. She brushed a tendril of wayward hair off her forehead with the back of her wrist and then continued cutting the cubes of squash.

"That sounds very formal, considering I'm just slouched over the counter watching you do your kitchen magic." Betty sat up straighter, perhaps nudged by the content of her own comment.

Mist divided the butternut cubes into two large roasting pans.

"I could help with the salad or the dessert," Betty suggested.

Mist smiled. "Both are already finished and waiting in the downstairs refrigerator. I made the chocolate caramel tart yesterday and put the salad together during part of the time when the guests were decorating the gingerbread house. I'll sprinkle pomegranate seeds on it just before we put it on the buffet. The dessert needs to stand at room temperature for about thirty minutes before we serve it. We'll pull it out of the refrigerator when guests begin to arrive."

"How many do you think we'll have this year?" Betty asked. She turned her head and smiled as Clive came in the back door and discarded his work gloves.

"Quite a few townsfolk are away visiting family this year," Mist said. "I estimate we'll have around fifty, including the hotel guests."

"I hope you made more than one tart," Clive said. "I just worked up an appetite bringing in that firewood."

Betty laughed. She already knew the answer. She stood, walked over to the side counter, and poured a mug of coffee.

"Of course." Mist smiled as she looked up. "I made four—two with extra chocolate drizzled on top."

"I'm ready anytime," Clive said. As Betty handed him the coffee, he gave her a peck on the cheek and stood beside her.

"Did I hear talk of chocolate tart?" Michael said from the interior doorway. "I could use something to keep up with Nigel. Thank goodness he agreed to a short break. Maybe your chocolate tart has a magical chess finesse ingredient, Mist?"

"Let me see." Mist closed her eyes and feigned concentration. "I don't recall immediately." She opened her eyes again. "I'll have to check the recipe. I may have accidentally substituted checkers chicanery instead."

Betty stood up and linked her arm through Clive's. "Michael, why don't you stay and help Mist while I go over to Clive's gallery with him."

"I wasn't planning…"

"Yes, you were," Betty said, squeezing Clive's arm tighter and giving him a look. "To set up for your after-Christmas sale, remember?"

"Ah, yes," Clive said. He raised his eyebrows, pleased with the idea as if it were his and not one Betty made up in the moment. He took a gulp of coffee and carried the mug to the sink.

"It's an easy job," Betty said, turning back to Michael. "You simply slouch over the counter and drink coffee."

Michael laughed. "I think I can handle that." He took over Betty's seat as the senior couple donned coats, hats, and gloves and went out the side door.

"Betty understated your role in helping me," Mist said. She added butter, cranberries, and seasoning to the butternut squash, set the dishes aside, covered. Moving soundlessly to the side counter, she poured a mug of coffee for Michael.

"Is that so?" Michael smiled as Mist placed the coffee in front of him, and allowed his fingertips to brush against hers as he reached for the mug. "It sounded so easy."

"It is easy," Mist said. "It requires no effort on your part. You help by simply being here. Everyone who passes through helps in some way; each person inspires me."

"What if I'd like to be more inspiring than others?" Michael leaned forward and sipped his coffee.

"Perhaps you are," Mist said. The back of her neck grew warm, and she changed the subject. "How are your chess games going with the professor?"

"I can't keep up with him." Michael shook his head. "Maybe you're feeding him the chess finesse ingredient, and I'm only getting the… what was that, exactly? Checkers chicanery?"

"I believe I stand wrongly accused," Mist said.

"All right, I take it back." Michael laughed. "But I will admit I'm envious of Nigel."

"For his chess ability?"

"Well, yes, it's admirable," Michael said. "He's quite the pro. But that's not the only reason. I also envy his new job."

"And why is that?"

"He'll be close to Timberton, since he'll be teaching here in Montana," Michael said. "He could manage weekend trips to the hotel here if he wanted."

"I suppose he *will* be a little closer than you will be in Louisiana," Mist said, teasing him.

"Just a bit," Michael said. He stood, finished his coffee, and set the mug in the sink before heading back to the chess game. As he passed behind Mist, he leaned in and whispered. "But not as close as I am now."

ELEVEN

Mist pulled a sprig of holly out of a table arrangement and reinserted it at a different angle. She stood back, satisfied. The clear glass cubes on each table in the café looked elegant with their mix of white tulips and paperwhites, yet cheerful with the accompanying bursts of red orchids, winterberries, and holly.

The buffet centerpiece, rather than being more elaborate, matched the table decorations, the only difference being multiples: a row of glass cubes ran across the back of the serving area. Votive candles, evergreen branches, and pine cones filled the spaces between each floral cube, scattered in what appeared to be random fashion, but was intentional.

Despite the day's busy schedule, Mist had not felt rushed. Nor did any chore drag out too long. She'd also found spaces of peacefulness between tasks. Betty had taken over in the kitchen, which allowed Mist to ponder the miniature paintings she planned to give guests in the morning, as well as to dress for the dinner.

Now, with the door to the café closed, she stood alone in a simple, forest-green dress that blended in with tablecloths of similar colors. The empire-waist cut allowed the washed silk fabric to flow gently down to her midcalf. Ballet flats exposed slender ankles usually hidden by her trademark work boots. A red orchid nestled in her braided hair at the nape of her neck, and vintage marcasite earrings dangled above her shoulders.

Mist moved from table to table, lighting candles, enjoying the glow as each flame took hold and reflected in already filled crystal glasses of ice water. She could hear the crowd gathering in the front parlor. The muffled chatter of hotel guests and townsfolk mingled with soft Christmas music. These moments, before this particular holiday meal, were among Mist's favorites. It soothed her spirit to know people would come together shortly over a special dinner.

"Ready?" Betty spoke softly from the kitchen doorway, understanding how much Mist enjoyed this brief ritual of quiet before she invited everyone in. "Clive, Maisie and Marge are here to help."

"Yes," Mist said as she lit the last of the candles on the buffet. "Let's bring everything out, and then invite the guests in."

Betty opened the kitchen door wide and held it as Clive carried in hearty platters of rosemary-orange roasted chicken and cherry-glazed pork loin. Maisie followed with the crisp, chilled salad, and Marge brought out overflowing baskets of warm cheddar chive biscuits, setting them at the end of the buffet, a crock of whipped butter alongside. Betty then followed, adding the side dishes of butternut squash and sautéed mushrooms. After a quick glance at the decadent spread and nearby beverage buffet, which Clive set up earlier, Mist nodded her approval.

"It looks wonderful." She thanked all who had helped set up the holiday meal and opened the front café doors wide. "Your Christmas Eve dinner is served," she announced.

Mist stepped aside, pleased, as the eager crowd flowed in and chose seats at tables around the enchanting room. Poppy, Hanna, and Jo sat together again, their parents at a table close enough to supervise, yet far enough away to allow the girls independence. Michael sat with Clara and Andrew, making sure to save a seat for Mist, who did, on Christmas Eve, allow herself to sit and enjoy the meal with guests, though usually only after some prodding.

Clayton arrived with his parents and joined Maisie at a table near the buffet. Betty had insisted on this, telling Maisie that "eating for two" was the perfect excuse to sit near the food. Mist and Betty both knew Maisie wouldn't be able to resist jumping up periodically to refill the buffet despite their attempts to tell her not to, so the table choice was practical, as well.

Marge, Millie, Sally, and other townsfolk scattered throughout the café with their families and friends. William Guthrie, of infamous "Wild Bill's" greasy spoon fame, showed up in fancy Western attire. Mist smiled at the sight of a red carnation boutonniere on his fringed leather jacket. Maisie had told her a week before that he'd ordered it for the occasion.

Glenda, from the Curl 'n Cue, sat with Ernie, the night bartender from Pop's Parlor. The town's oddly adjoining beauty salon and combination bar and pool parlor had created a good friendship between the two.

Mist encouraged everyone to eat all they'd like but didn't want them to feel obliged to try everything. She knew people had different preferences and dietary needs. It came as no surprise that Bill Guthrie filled his plate with extra chicken and pork while Millie made a main dish out of the pear, brie, and pomegranate salad, accompanied by butternut squash and cheddar chive biscuits. In keeping with this philosophy, she'd prepared a fruit and cheese plate to bring out when the chocolate tart was served. She believed it was always good to offer choices, especially since Moonglow had no menus even on "regular" days.

As Mist floated from table to table, guests filled plates at the buffet and returned to their seats, starting up conversations with each other.

"Your garage is bigger than mine." Clara pointed this out to Andrew as Mist paused to take the saved seat at their table. "So there's more storage room."

"True," Andrew said as he stuck a fork through a cube of butternut squash and then topped it off with a cranberry. "But do we really need storage room? I'm all for getting rid of things we don't use."

Sally leaned over from the next table. "Trust me; your local thrift store will be happy to take those items off your hands. I'm always excited to see new things come into Second Hand Sally's. And other people are happy to find them."

Mist sat down in the saved seat next to Michael, relaxed but poised, her hands folded and resting in her lap as she listened to the debate. "Less is more," she said quietly. Her voice barely registered above the surrounding conversation, but those at the table heard her.

"Yes," Michael said. "It's true. Look at how little we have with us here in Timberton, yet we lack for nothing. We're just used to having our possessions around us at home."

"Well, I'd gladly get rid of my pots and pans if Mist would come home with me and cook every night," Clara said. "But I doubt the people of Timberton would appreciate my taking her away."

"And you'd need to bring her back every Christmas," Andrew added.

"Yes," Michael said. "Too many people would miss her."

"I'd sure miss her," Bill Guthrie piped up, waiving a biscuit in the air.

"You're not going anywhere, are you, Mist?" Clive frowned. He'd only heard part of the conversation as he delivered a drink refill to a guest.

Mist smiled. "Of course not, Clive. This is my home." Michael reached over and took her hand. She kept her eyes focused on the others at the table but did not pull her hand away.

"We're just talking about getting rid of things we don't need," Clara said.

"Downsizing," Andrew added. "I believe that's the current term."

A burst of giggles erupted from the girls' table. Mist turned toward them and smiled. All three were hunched forward, more intent on whispering than eating.

"Something about a cute guy they all like in a new band," Clive explained. "I heard them when I walked by."

"They grow up so quickly," Clara said. "We all do. I remember being that age as if it were just a few years ago, not decades."

"And what cute boy musician would you have been giggling about back then?" Andrew asked. Everyone at the table watched Clara.

"Oh, that's easy. *That* cute boy musician was Elvis," Clara said. "Though Frankie Avalon was right up there too." She glanced shyly at Andrew, as if she'd just divulged her secret past.

Betty passed the table and paused. "Mist, you should eat something. How about letting me fix you a small plate from the buffet?"

"I'm fine, but thank you." Mist stood up, surprising herself when she released Michael's hand, as if she hadn't realized they'd been touching at all until that moment. "I nibbled earlier. I want to be sure the guests are taken care of right now."

"There's no use arguing with you," Betty said, smiling. She moved on to other tables, picking up dishes from those who were finished and encouraging other diners to go back for seconds.

As Mist moved toward the kitchen, she stopped at tables along the way and listened to the talk among guests. The professor and Rolf discussed current events while Chloe and Greta weighed the pros and cons of moving versus remodeling. Maisie nodded politely while Clayton's mother disbursed parenting advice as Clayton attempted to remind his mother that the child had yet to be born. Millie encouraged Glenda and Marge to participate in an upcoming fundraiser for local schools to be held at the library in mid-January. Gift certificates for the local beauty parlor and candy store would be a good draw for the event's raffle.

Maisie stepped into the kitchen. "Oh, please, Mist, let me serve the dessert."

"Of course!" This would give Maisie a good reason to escape the parenting discussion, and Mist had one more mission she felt pulled to accomplish. All the talk of houses and homes over dinner had left Mist thinking about Hollister. Although he had come to accept Room Seven as his own, almost always slipping in the back door and staying overnight, she doubted he would ever come to a community meal. The answer to this conundrum was simple: she would take the meal to him. Not just the leftovers she always placed in the refrigerator in his room each time she served other people who dined at Moonglow, but an actual holiday meal, decorations and all.

Mist pulled a wicker tray from a slim cabinet below the kitchen counter and set it on the center island. She prepared a plate from the buffet, covered it with foil, and placed it in the center of the tray. Above the plate, she set a faux candle with an LED light and battery in a votive that matched those in the dining area. She then arranged evergreen strands and pine cones to the sides of the votive holder, placed silverware elegantly on a red linen napkin, and took the tray downstairs.

"Was Hollister there?" Betty asked when Mist returned to the kitchen.

"Not yet," Mist said. "But he will be."

"When?" Betty asked, puzzled by Mist's certainty.

"When he's ready to come home," Mist said. "We all come home when we're ready."

"And until then?" Betty asked.

Mist pointed to the chocolate tarts, ready for the dinner's finale. "Until then, we enjoy dessert."

TWELVE

"It's amazing."

"I've never seen anything quite like it."

"What a fantastic idea."

Mist stood in the archway, watching. Long after the chocolate tart had been served and dinner dishes put away, the crowd of townsfolk and hotel guests lingered in the front parlor. Adults sipped coffee, brandy, or both while the younger crowd stirred hot chocolate with long peppermint sticks. Marge and Glenda admired the display of pomanders in a basket on a low table. Jo showed hers off to the ladies, explaining how she'd poked holes in the orange in order to insert the whole cloves. Rolf, an accomplished pianist, rolled out one carol after the next as those with voices both fair and not so fair belted out lyrics to old-time favorites.

"It's really wonderful!"

"Like a fairy tale."

"So clever, so creative!"

Throughout the evening, no matter how impressed people were with the exquisite tree, the seasonal music, and the overall joyful atmosphere in general, one thing dominated it all: the gingerbread house.

"I just want to take a big bite out of it," William Guthrie said. He'd exchanged his fringed jacket for a popcorn-and-cranberry garland from the Christmas tree and looked as festive as everyone else.

Clayton, who'd stayed at the hotel with Maisie after his parents retired to his house, chuckled. "I don't recommend it, Bill. Not unless you have a good dentist." A round of laughter followed.

Clive put his hand on Bill's shoulder. "Better take his advice. There's plenty of solid wood hiding under that gingerbread, and a few tough nails, as well."

"I don't know," Rolf called over from the piano. "Maybe he should try it out. We could all sing along." Pounding out a short introduction on the piano, he soon had the entire room singing "All I Want for Christmas is My Two Front Teeth." Those who weren't singing were laughing or patting Bill sympathetically on the back.

"Very funny," Bill said, laughing too. "I'll stick to Betty's glazed cinnamon nuts. Those are safer."

"And delicious," Greta said, directing her comment to Betty, who stood near the Christmas tree, half exploring, half hesitating to look too far inside the branches. "I meant to ask for the recipe, if you're willing to share it, Betty."

"Of course!" Betty said immediately. She turned toward Greta quickly, as if caught doing something forbidden. "It's so easy to make and great for little gifts. I'll send a copy of the recipe home with you."

Michael, who had been sitting near the fireplace, as usual, walked over to the arched doorway and stood by Mist, a conspiratorial smile on his face as he lowered his voice and spoke. "Is Betty doing what I think she's doing?"

"Definitely," Mist said. "I've seen her by the tree three times. He hid it well this year."

Clive's custom-made ornament for Betty had become a tradition. He never let on in advance what it would be. Only people who'd seen the ornaments from previous years had clues, and those were few: it would be silver, with a Yogo sapphire in it somewhere, and it would be a different design from previous years.

"Give me a hint," Michael said. "You and Clive are good friends. You must have an idea what this year's ornament will be."

Mist gave Michael a look of mock disapproval. "Why, Michael Blanton, you should know I wouldn't divulge an important secret like that, even if I knew!"

Michael leaned closer. "Ah, I see... Does that mean you *don't* know?"

Mist smiled. "I didn't say that."

Michael propped his arm against the archway in front of Mist. "Then you do know."

"I didn't say that either."

Mist ducked under Michael's arm and slipped away, laughing.

Betty had curbed her curiosity and stepped away from the Christmas tree. Hanna, Poppy, and Jo all sat inside the gingerbread house, taking turns poking their heads out to see what the adults were up to. There was enough holiday spirit in the hotel to fill a town ten times the size of Timberton.

Rolf started to slow the tempo of the musical selections, calming the crowd with a medley of "Silent Night" and "Away in a Manger." A few guests stood near the piano, others wandered away to enjoy the music from one of the room's cozy seats.

Hanna and Jo emerged from the gingerbread house and headed for a basket of cookies, each choosing one before exploring the ornaments on the tree. Noticing that Poppy remained inside the sweet structure, Mist approached it, lifted her skirt just enough to be able to kneel down without pulling the fabric, and looked inside. Poppy sat in a back corner, staring at the floor. "Mind if I join you? If you'd rather be alone, that's fine too. Sometimes I like to be alone, so I'll understand."

Poppy looked up. "Come on in."

Mist crawled in and sat in the opposite corner. She took a deep breath and exhaled. "My, this house smells good—like licorice and peppermint."

Poppy nodded. "I love it. I want to stay in here."

"Tonight, you mean?" Mist thought quickly, doubting the professor and Chloe would go for the idea.

"No," Poppy said, shaking her head. "I want this to be my *real* house."

"But you'll be getting a new house soon," Mist said, watching the girl. "And I'll bet it's bigger than this one. Just a guess, you know…" Mist let her voice trail off, as if pondering this thought.

Poppy laughed, and Mist was relieved. "Of course it will be."

"I think that will be more comfortable, don't you?" Mist said. "I can't quite see more than one person living in this house."

"It *would* be crowded." Poppy pretended to take Mist seriously for a moment. But she lost heart and looked dejected again. "I don't want a new house. I want my old one. My room was just the way I wanted it to be. I like that we get to stay with Uncle Nigel a while, but I wish we could have just stayed in England."

"Change can be difficult," Mist said. "And this is a big one for you: new country, new school, new friends, and a new home."

"We don't even have one yet," Poppy said. "I'm tired of staying in hotels, though I like *yours*. What if we don't find a good house?"

"Oh, you will," Mist said without hesitation.

"How do you know?

"Sometimes I just know things," Mist said. "I can almost see it... at least I think I can see your room... What is that on your desk?"

"My computer," Poppy said. "Mum said I could have my own computer so I can email my friends in England and they can email me back."

"Ah." Mist nodded. "That's what I thought. And what's on your bed?"

"That's Figgy," Poppy said.

"Figgy? Tell me about Figgy." Mist waited.

"He's a sock monkey," Poppy said. "I've had him since I was little."

"How did he get his name?" Mist asked.

"I know it's silly, but I just liked it because it sounded funny." Poppy smiled.

"That's a perfect reason." Mist nodded again and then tilted her head, thinking. "So how would you get that desk, bed, computer, and Figgy in here?" She looked around the four-by-four interior of the gingerbread house.

Poppy sighed. "You're right. I guess I'll have to be patient."

Mist smiled. "That sounds like a good plan."

Chloe stuck her head in the doorway. "There you are, Poppy. What are you two discussing so seriously?"

"We're talking about my room in our new house, Mum, how Figgy will be right there on the bed in my room," Poppy said. "Mist says she sees it."

"Ah," Chloe said. "Well, I think you and Figgy will have that soon. Uncle Nigel has several places in mind. He did some searching online while we were still in England. We're going to go look at them right after Christmas, and you can come along to help us choose which house will be best."

Poppy lit up. "Okay!" She started to leave but paused. Turning to Mist impulsively, she threw her arms around her in a fierce hug and then crawled out of the structure.

"Well. That's unusual," Chloe said. "She's at that age where she only wants a hug when she has a bellyache or some boy she likes doesn't like her back. You must have the right kind of magic. Thank you."

Chloe scooted out of the house to join Poppy in the main room.

Before Mist could crawl out of the house, Jo ducked in, followed by Hanna.

"Poppy says you know what the room in her new house is going to look like," Hanna said, a skeptical look on her face.

"News travels fast," Mist said but understood the three girls had a new kind of quickly whispered communication that almost needed no words.

"She doesn't even have a new house yet!" Jo exclaimed. She was almost short enough to stand straight inside the gingerbread house, and she put her hands on her hips to emphasize her point.

"That's true," Mist said. "But we don't always have to see things up close to imagine them."

"So what do you see in our rooms?" Hanna said.

Mist thought a minute before speaking. "I see bright colors, a lively environment, though not extreme, just invigorating.

"In… vig…" Jo frowned, trying to repeat the five syllable word.

"Invigorating," Mist repeated.

"In-vi-go-ra-ting." Jo glowed as she spoke the word successfully. "What's it mean?"

"Giving you energy."

"Like a magical zap!" Jo's face lit up.

"Yes," Mist said. "That's a good way to put it: bright colors to give you a magical zap of energy. Thank you, Jo. I will think of it like that now."

"We just have boring stuff in the room now, nothing bright. What else do you see?" Hanna asked. "Besides this weird zap stuff you guys are talking about." She sat cross-legged and propped her elbows on her knees, resting her chin in her hands.

Mist closed her eyes, not for dramatic effect but to verify what she believed she saw before stating it. When she opened them, she said, "I see two beds."

"That can't be right," Hanna said. "They want to build another room. So we'll only have one bed in each room."

"Yeah," Jo added, her voice lacking enthusiasm.

Mist nodded. "Yes, I heard about that. But I still see two beds." She paused. "Do you two want your own rooms?"

Hanna and Jo exchanged looks. Jo moved closer to Hanna and sat down beside her. Hanna put her arm around her younger sister. "We used to beg Mom and Dad for our own rooms," Hanna said, and Mist thought she saw tears in her eyes.

Jo sat next to her sister and headbutted her shoulder. "Now we kind of want to share. So we can talk and stuff."

"I see," Mist said. "Maybe that is why I see two beds."

"One room with bright colors," Jo said. "That sounds rad."

Hanna rolled her eyes. "*Nobody* says 'rad,' Jo."

"Maybe they do." Mist laughed. "Maybe rad is an easier way to say invigorating."

Greta stuck her head into the gingerbread house. "There you girls are. It's getting late. I'd say another ten minutes and then bed. Clive is calling everyone over to the Christmas tree."

"All right," Hanna said. She turned to Jo. "Let's go see." The two girls crawled out, Mist right behind them.

"It looked nice and cozy in there," Greta said. She smiled as Mist stood up and straightened her skirt.

"Yes, very," Mist said. "Especially after we rearranged the furniture." She left Greta peering inside the empty gingerbread house, a puzzled look on her face.

Mist found Clive by the Christmas tree, ready to reveal the special ornament he'd designed for Betty, who stood beside him, blushing at the attention from the small crowd that had gathered. Clive reached through the trees branches to a section in the rear that was thick enough to hide this year's small treasure. He pulled it out and handed it to Betty.

"Oh, Clive!" Betty exclaimed. "It's beautiful!" She held the ornament up for everyone to see. A sterling silver wreath dangled from a satin ribbon. Tiny red sapphires dotted the wreath in haphazard locations, giving the impression of sparkling berries.

"It looks like the wreath we made on the gingerbread house," Jo said. "Except you can't eat this one." A soft round of laughter followed her comment.

"I just love Christmas Eve," Clara said. She and Andrew stood near the tree, arm in arm. The other guests agreed.

"It's a special evening," Betty said, "thanks to all of you for being here with us."

"Special, indeed," the professor said. "Which we owe to you and Mist, Betty." He paused and then grinned. "And even to you, Clive." Again, laughter filled the room.

Mist watched as Betty hung the silver wreath back on the tree, this time in the front. Guests settled back into conversation with each other. Greta and Chloe escorted the girls to bed. Michael smiled across the room at Mist, who smiled in return before quietly excusing herself for the evening. Her day's work may have appeared finished to others, but she knew it wasn't. Miniature canvases and paint awaited her late-night attention.

Back in her room, Mist looked at the four-by-four squares of canvas attached to her easel, grateful Clive had created clips to hold the tiny frames. Sales of her miniature paintings had continued to increase over the past year. It was useful to be able to work on multiples at once. This evening, it would be particularly helpful.

Moving to her paint supplies, she pulled out not just soft colors, as she often did, but the liveliest: bright red, cornflower blue, deep orange, sunshine yellow, and a medium green. The vibrant colors awakened her creative spirit, providing renewed energy after the long day. *Invigorating*, she thought. Then she chuckled to herself. *Rad.*

Two hours later, Mist stood back, looked at the finished paintings, and smiled. Satisfied her parting gifts for the guests conveyed what she wanted, she slipped into bed.

THIRTEEN

Christmas day dawned with sunlight slipping through newly falling snow, creating a magical ambiance perfect for the holiday morning. Mist rose early and set up the coffee and tea service in the lobby. She put on Christmas carols at a decibel not high enough to wake the guests but just loud enough to welcome them when they eventually entered the main hotel area. As she returned to the kitchen, Betty joined her from the back hallway.

"Merry Christmas, Mist." Betty's red chenille bathrobe featured an embroidered snowman just below the left collar, with matching designs on each of two large pockets.

"And the same to you, Betty." Mist smiled at Betty, and then turned as the back door opened. Clive stepped inside. "And the same to *you*, Clive."

"The same what?" Clive asked as he removed his jacket and brushed snow off his head.

"Why, the same good morning wish for a merry Christmas, of course," Betty said. She poured a mug of coffee and handed it to Clive.

"Gingerbread pancakes, right?" Clive said, eyeing a large pitcher of batter on the counter.

"That's the plan," Mist said.

"I'm ready to start flipping anytime."

"Clive, I dare say you flipped a long time ago," Betty said, elbowing him. Clive laughed along with Betty and Mist. The women appreciated Clive's recent habit of helping with breakfast, especially on mornings after a complicated dinner. "Do I hear footsteps on the stairway already?" Betty said, ears twitching. "This early?"

"And giggling?" Clive added.

Mist nodded. It would have been far more surprising if the girls had *not* scurried down to study the Christmas tree. Mist had noticed when she glanced into the front parlor as she set up the coffee area that a few gifts had arrived beneath the tree at some point during the night, compliments of sneaky adults.

The sounds of the girls' voices diminished as others began to emerge from their rooms into the front parlor, where Clive was lighting a fire. Warm beverages, a warm fire, and the warm lights of the Christmas tree surrounded the guests.

Soon the smell of gingerbread enhanced the scene. By the time Mist opened the doors to the café, most guests had already gathered downstairs. They flowed in to choose their seats and filled their plates with pancakes, some topped with butter and syrup and others with fresh berries and whipped cream. Clive fried up eggs for those who wanted them, and Betty refilled coffee mugs and juice glasses for those who desired more. The centerpieces on the table from the previous night created a combination of casual and elegant that was perfect for the holiday breakfast.

"Ah," Rolf said with an appreciative smile on his face. "Real maple syrup."

"Nothing like it," Andrew said. Clara, sitting next to him, nodded.

Jo practically bounced up and down in her chair, already finished with her breakfast. "When do we get to open presents?" she asked. Hanna and Poppy also waited expectantly for the answer.

"After breakfast," Greta said.

"Let's just enjoy the meal first," Chloe said. She and Greta exchanged smiles, knowing it wasn't so easy for children to do the things adults so casually said they should do.

The girls sighed. Hanna and Poppy finished their food while Jo continued to bounce and look toward the front parlor.

"I remember being that excited when I was a child," Michael said.

"Were you the type to sneak a peek at presents before Christmas day?" the professor asked. "I had a cousin who would find presents weeks ahead of time, open them, and then rewrap them."

"He was quite clever, especially since he got away with it," Chloe said. "But I wouldn't have done it. I prefer surprises."

"I don't think his parents ever knew," the professor said.

"He must have been careful when unwrapping and rewrapping the packages," Greta said.

"Indeed. He was meticulous. I don't know how he managed."

"I can barely wrap a gift to begin with." Clara laughed. "It's a good thing Andrew and I agreed not to exchange them."

"The best gifts aren't always wrapped in paper," Mist said softly as she passed the table. "They sometimes appear as mystery, adventure, forgiveness, or joy, for example. Even adversity." Several people nodded, others simply pondered her words as they finished the last bites of their meals.

"Now?" Jo asked. She sent a pleading look toward the adults.

"Or hope," Greta said to Rolf and the rest of her table companions before turning to Jo. "Yes, you and your sister may go on in and sit by the tree, but do not open anything yet."

"You too, Poppy," Chloe said, and all three girls scampered away.

"I believe I'm ready to retire to the front room as well," the professor said, standing.

"I'll join you," Michael said, "but no chess this morning, please."

"Agreed," the professor said. "I would feel a bit cheeky defeating you on this lovely Christmas day." Both laughed as they headed to the front room.

Soon the others followed, and the glow of the fire, the sweet scent of the gingerbread house, and the enticing lights and ornaments on the tree drew them together. Once the adults joined them, Hanna, Jo, and Poppy eagerly opened presents brought from home: holiday pajamas, new books, a bracelet for one, a glittery headband for another, and a variety of other items that pleased each girl. Greta and Rolf exchanged small gifts, as did the professor and Chloe. Clara and Andrew looked on, satisfied to witness the joy of the moment.

As the families finished exchanging gifts, Mist reached beneath the tree and pulled out four packages, each wrapped in burgundy velvet and tied with gold ribbon. Rather than hand them out individually, to be opened one by one, as she had on other Christmas mornings, she handed them all out at the same time: one to Clara and Andrew, one to Rolf, Greta, Hanna and Jo, one to the professor, Chloe and Poppy, and one to Michael.

"What's this?" Rolf asked. He and Greta exchanged looks, grateful yet puzzled.

Clara spoke up. "Mist is full of surprises for her Christmas guests."

"Charming surprises," Michael said. He shook the package next to his ear, as if checking to see what it might be, though he'd experienced Mist's Christmas-morning tradition twice already and knew shaking would reveal nothing.

Clive, watching from the archway, grinned. "Mist, I do believe I saw you roll your eyes when Michael shook that package."

Mist looked at Clive. "I do not roll my eyes." But she smiled, knowing he'd caught her teasing response to Michael. "We can't always believe everything we see."

"Or see everything we believe," Michael said.

"Yes, yes," the professor agreed. "Very true."

"Should we open these now?" Clara said. "Who should go first?"

"There's no need for anyone to go first or last or in any order at all," Mist said. "It's just a little something to take home with you."

"Let's let the girls open it." Greta gave the package to Hanna and Jo.

The professor and Chloe handed their package to Poppy. As the girls pulled the ribbon and fabric off the gifts, Clara and Andrew did the same, as did Michael. Everyone smiled as the miniature paintings were unveiled.

"It's the gingerbread house!" Poppy held up her family's painting for everyone to see.

"Same here," Jo said, showing off a similar canvas.

"It looks just like the hotel's gingerbread house," Hanna said.

"How lovely," Clara said. She and Andrew had opened theirs together and now held it up. Michael did the same with his.

"What a wonderful gift, Mist!" Greta said. "How clever of you to give us identical houses so we can remember the one we decorated here together." The other adults agreed while Mist quietly watched the three girls comparing their gifts.

"Wait," Poppy said, looking closely first at the painting she held and then at the one in Jo's hands. "They're not exactly the same. See, Hanna?" She pointed to the doorways in the two paintings. You have two beds inside your house, right next to each other."

"So we can be close together," Hanna said, giving Jo a big-sister hug. "Or…" She paused, and both girls looked at their parents, smiles fading. "It might be one for each room."

"Are you saying… you'd rather share a room?" Greta looked at Rolf and then back at the girls.

"Could we?" Jo said. "Could we share a room? I'd miss Hanna if she slept in a different place."

"Can we please?" Hanna added.

"Of course you can," Rolf said, and Greta nodded. "We can save building the extra room for another time."

"What's in your house, Poppy?" Hanna said.

"It looks like a table with… three teacups on it," Poppy said.

"What's that under the table," Jo asked.

Poppy squinted at the table. "That's Figgy!" she squealed.

The professor and Chloe laughed. "Well," the professor said, "I can't imagine a better home than one with three cups for English tea, plus a sock monkey."

"This is brilliant, Mist," Chloe said.

Mist smiled, knowing the home would be made of much more than canvas and paint.

"Look closely at ours, Andrew." Clara held the painting while Andrew fished his reading glasses out of his shirt pocket.

"There's nothing inside," Andrew said, looking first at Mist and then at Clara.

"But look at the outside," Clara said, pointing to a spot next to the door.

"Looks like a key hanging on a hook," Andrew said. "A shiny key."

Clara nodded. "Yes, as if it's brand-new."

"An empty house with a shiny new key…" Andrew mused. "There's an idea. Instead of choosing between our two houses…"

"We could sell both houses and downsize into something new," Clara said. "I hadn't even thought of that."

"A new beginning in a new home," Andrew said. "It's something to consider." He put his arm around Clara's shoulders as she turned toward the one person who had not said anything so far.

"What about yours?" Clara asked Michael. "Can you see anything inside the house?"

"As a matter of fact, I can," Michael said, looking at his painting closely. "I see a fireplace, a chair, and a small table with a stack of books."

"Sounds like that would make it a home for you," Greta said. "I've seen how much you love to sit by the fire and read."

"Reading is a passion of mine," Michael said. "I can't remember a time when I wasn't intrigued by an unopened book, even as a child. The pages inside always represent something: knowledge or mystery or another world altogether. That's why I chose to teach literature, because I love to read."

"Hear, hear," the professor said. "My motivation, as well."

"So the home in your painting is in New Orleans," Rolf said.

"For now," Michael said. "But I've applied to a few different universities lately, so we'll see. But wherever I go, there will be books."

Betty glanced at Mist, whose shoulders rose slightly. Had anyone else made the movement, it wouldn't even pass as a shrug. Yet coming from Mist it indicated Michael's interest in other teaching positions was news to her.

"Well," Clive said. "I'm about ready to build a good snowman." He rubbed his hands together in anticipation.

"I want to help," Jo said, jumping up. Hanna and Poppy rose as well.

"Jackets, girls," Greta said.

"And mittens and hats," Chloe added.

"My vote is for a lazy day," Rolf said as the girls ran off for their outdoor attire. Some of the adults seemed to share his enthusiasm for resting.

Mist silently agreed. The past few days had been hectic. A little down time would be relaxing for everyone, guests and hosts alike.

"I believe I'll make some hot chocolate to go with everyone's lazy day," Mist said. "It will be out in the lobby, along with a tray of cookies." Heading for the kitchen, she couldn't help but smile. The guests were content, and a peaceful day stretched ahead.

FOURTEEN

Betty took a sip of coffee and looked across the kitchen's center island at Mist. "This is one of my favorite *and* least favorite afternoons."

Mist nodded, her hands wrapped around a mug of green tea. "I understand. The day after Christmas feels like something special is over, yet it's also the beginning of something new: the stretch into the new year."

"I was sorry to see the Webers leave so early this morning," Betty said. "But they had an early flight, so they had no choice. I thought they'd have to drag Jo out of the gingerbread house though."

"So true." Mist smiled. "She really didn't want to leave."

"And the professor, Chloe, and Poppy left right after brunch," Betty said. "Speaking of brunch, Clive didn't come by. It's not like him to miss a meal."

"I wouldn't worry," Mist said. "I saw him sneak in for coffee this morning. And three blueberry scones were missing right after that, from the tray I had just set out."

"I doubt he went hungry then." Betty laughed.

"No, I'm sure he didn't," Mist agreed.

"Interesting how everyone arrived the same day this year, and are leaving the same day," Betty said.

"Each year is different," Mist said. "It will always be that way and always a surprise. We never know what changes time will bring."

"At least those families have the miniature paintings you gave them," Betty said. "That was a clever idea."

"It seemed appropriate. They all worked on the house together, and they all face decisions about their living situations." Mist sipped her tea and put the mug down. "Now they've had a chance to look inside and think about what they want, what they need."

"I hope this hotel will be their Christmas home for years to come, regardless of where they settle during the rest of the time," Betty said.

"Some will return, and some won't." Mist's words lingered in the air like wind deciding whether to change direction or not.

"Clara and Andrew will be back, I think," Betty said. "She's been spending Christmas here for years."

"Yes, they plan to come back." Clive's voice surprised them. Buried in thought, they hadn't noticed him appear in the kitchen doorway. "At least that's what they said. They're in the front hallway getting ready to leave."

"Well, look who decided to show up," Betty said as she stood. "We should go see Clara and Andrew off." Mist followed Betty to the lobby, picking up a small cellophane bag of cookies on the counter on her way out of the kitchen.

"Wonderful," Andrew said as Mist handed him the package. "I can't get enough of Timberton's cookies."

"I hope you'll come back for more next year," Betty said.

"We plan to." Clara hugged Betty and then Mist.

Goodbyes said, Clive helped carry their luggage out to their rental car.

"So we have one guest left," Betty said.

"Yes, so we do." Mist moved to the archway, looked into the front parlor, and then turned back to Betty. "He's not in his usual reading spot. Are you certain he didn't already leave?" Mist felt a featherlight catch in her voice as she spoke.

"Maybe he's packing," Betty offered as Clive came back inside.

"Are you talking about Michael?" Clive said. "He went out for a walk, down toward the gallery, I think." He looked at Mist, dressed in a long skirt and light gauze-type tunic. "It's kinda chilly out, so bundle up if you decide to go out too. You know, for example, if you decided to go for a walk or something." He winked at Betty, a gesture Mist didn't miss.

"Perhaps I will," Mist said. "Since you suggested it…" She disappeared briefly and reappeared in her heavy, hooded cape, wearing an old-fashioned hand muff with a thick fur texture.

"That thing's not alive, is it?" Clive teased her.

"It's faux fur, Clive," Betty said, laughing.

Mist paused on her way to the door. "You never know. Life is unpredictable." She extended the muff quickly toward Clive and then pulled it back in one smooth move, causing him to jump. Leaving Betty and Clive in near hysterics, she headed for the gallery, grinning mischievously all the way.

The street was almost empty as Mist walked toward the gallery, since most residents of the small town were enjoying a day at home with family. Knowing Clive had decided to stay closed for a holiday break after Christmas, she expected to find Michael ambling somewhere between the hotel and gallery or perhaps over in the town park. Instead, she was surprised to see the gallery lights on, although the CLOSED sign hung in the front window. As she approached, the lights went off, the door opened, and Michael stepped out. He pulled the door closed and turned, clearly happy to see Mist standing about ten yards away.

"Clive told me you had taken a walk in this direction," Mist said. "But the gallery is closed today, isn't it?"

Michael nodded. "Yes, but I needed to pick something up—something I ordered from him."

"You've only been here for a few days," Mist said. "When did you have time?"

"You've heard of phone calls and emails, haven't you?" Michael smiled and guided Mist across the street to a wrought iron bench in the park. He brushed snow off the seat, and they both sat down. "I spoke with him a few weeks ago. I wanted to give you something for Christmas and knew he was the perfect person to call."

Mist tilted her head. A few snowflakes fell on one cheek, and Michael gently brushed them off. "I must say you have me curious now," she said.

Michael reached in his jacket pocket and pulled out a silver chain. A charm dangled from the end, catching its own snowflakes.

"Oh!" Mist exclaimed. "It's beautiful!" She reached for the intricate pendant, a miniature of the sign that hung above the café. A perfect example of Clive's handiwork, the scripted word "Moonglow" was accentuated with a tiny Yogo sapphire.

"I couldn't decide what image to have him make at first," Michael said. "But with all the talk of 'home' this Christmas, I knew I'd made the right choice. The café is your home, Mist. It's where people gather, where you are able to touch people's lives." Unclasping the chain, he reached inside the hood of Mist's cape and fastened it securely around her neck. "There, it's perfect," he said.

"It's more than perfect. Thank you," Mist said. "And where is home for you, Michael? What's this talk about applying to other universities?"

"I may be ready for a change," Michael said. "So I thought I'd look into different opportunities."

"Such as?"

"Cambridge has an opening, for one," Michael said.

"Oh," Mist said. "Well, it's an excellent school. I understand wanting to look into it."

"There's also an opportunity at Pepperdine, in California."

"Opposite side of the country," Mist said. "Quite a difference. Anywhere else?"

Michael nodded. "Rutgers is another possibility."

"It sounds like east coast versus west coast," Mist noted.

"It almost is," Michael said.

"Almost?"

"Nigel says there's another opening at the University of Montana, aside from the one he is taking. I may look into it."

"Well, it's always good to have options," Mist said. She fought back a smile and pushed her hands deeper into the muff as a gust of wind blew through the town park.

"Let's walk back," Michael suggested. "The wind's picking up, and it's already cold." He pulled Mist's cape tighter around her to keep her warm. "And... I do need to get going."

"I know you do," Mist said, standing up. "Let's go."

"Wait," Michael said, "I'm forgetting something." Gently he lifted Mist's face toward his and kissed her. "There. Now we can go."

The short walk back to the hotel took only a few minutes and seemed even shorter. After multiple exchanges of gratitude and good wishes for safe travel, Michael left. Mist and Betty stood by the Christmas tree together, watching the snow fall outside on the empty street.

"What a wonderful Christmas," Betty said. "Special." She reached out and touched the silver wreath ornament Clive had given her.

"Yes," Mist said, her fingers touching the delicate charm near her neckline. "It was special. But then, they're all special, in different ways."

Mist took Betty's hand.

"I can see that," Betty mused. "Last year was special, too, and so was the year before. I suppose you're right."

"Of course I'm right." Mist laughed. "If you're still not sure, just wait until next year."

BETTY'S COOKIE EXCHANGE RECIPES

Glazed Cinnamon Nuts
Gingerbread Cookies
Cherry Pecan Holiday Cookies
Gingerbread-Eggnog Trifle
Homemade Eggnog
Cocoa Kisses
Lois Tallman's Ginger Snaps
Santa's Whiskers Cookies
Angel Crisp Cookies
Kourabiedes
Kitchen-Sink Cookies
Ginger Orange Cookies
Christmas Swirl Fudge
Grandma's Kringles
Vegan Sugar Cookies
Mint-Chocolate Macarons
Chocolate-Mint Ganache Filling
Easy Cookies
Khrustyky
Peanut Brittle
Swedish Coconut Cookies

GLAZED CINNAMON NUTS
(A family recipe)

Ingredients:

1 cup sugar
1/4 cup water
1/8 teaspoon cream of tartar
Heaping teaspoon of cinnamon
1 tablespoon butter
1 1/2 cups walnut halves

Directions:

Boil sugar, water, cream of tartar and cinnamon to soft ball stage (236 degrees.)

Remove from heat.

Add butter and walnuts.

Stir until walnuts separate.

Place on wax paper to cool.

GINGERBREAD COOKIES

(Submitted by Kim Davis, from her blog,
Cinnamon and Sugar and a Little Bit of Murder)

Ingredients:

8 ounces (2 sticks) unsalted butter, softened to room temperature
1 cup granulated sugar
2 large eggs
1/2 cup molasses
4 cups all-purpose flour
2 tablespoons cocoa powder
1 teaspoon salt
2 tablespoons ground ginger
1 tablespoon ground cinnamon
2 teaspoons cloves
1/2 teaspoon cayenne powder
1 teaspoon baking soda

Directions:

In a standing mixer, beat butter and sugar together at medium speed until fluffy. Add the eggs, one at a time, and beat until thoroughly combined, then mix in molasses.

In a separate bowl, whisk together the flour, cocoa, salt, spices, and baking soda, then slowly add to butter mixture, mixing on low speed until well combined.

Divide the dough into two portions and wrap well with plastic wrap. Refrigerate at least 8 hours or overnight.

On a lightly floured surface, roll the dough out 1/4 inch thick and cut out shapes using your favorite cookie cutters. Place on parchment lined baking sheets and bake at 350 degrees for 10–12 minutes or until lightly browned, rotating baking sheet halfway through. Cool cookies on baking sheet for five minutes, then finish cooling on a wire rack. Frost with your favorite icing and/or sprinkles.

CHERRY PECAN HOLIDAY COOKIES
(Submitted by Vera Kenyon)

Ingredients:

1/2 cup butter
1/2 cup margarine
1 cup powdered sugar
1 egg
1 teaspoon vanilla
2 1/4 cups flour
1 cup chopped pecans
4 or 6 ounces each: red and green candied cherries, chopped into
four pieces (cutting with kitchen scissors works well)

Directions:

Using an electric mixer, cream butter, margarine, sugar, egg, and
vanilla at medium speed until light and fluffy. At low speed, add
flour. Stir in chopped pecans.

Divide dough in half; add red chopped cherries to one half, green
cherries to the other half. Shape each half into a 2-inch-diameter
log. Wrap in waxed paper and chill for 4 hours or overnight.

Preheat oven to 350 degrees. Cut logs into 1/4-inch slices; place
2 inches apart on ungreased cookie sheets.

Bake for 8–10 minutes, until light golden brown.

Makes 4 1/2 dozen cookies. The cookies freeze well, so they are
great to make ahead.

GINGERBREAD-EGGNOG TRIFLE

(Submitted by Kim Davis, from her blog,
Cinnamon and Sugar and a Little Bit of Murder)

Ingredients:

1 (14.5 ounce) box gingerbread cake mix baked according to the package directions*
1 (5.1 ounce) box instant vanilla pudding mix
3 cups eggnog (store bought and low-fat version is fine) *Or use Homemade Eggnog recipe
1 tablespoon bourbon (optional)
2 (8 ounce) containers Cool Whip
Mini gingersnaps or gingerbread boy cookies for garnish (optional)

Directions:

Bake the cake mix according to package instructions. Cool completely before assembling the trifle.

Add pudding mix to a large bowl and whisk in the eggnog and bourbon if using. Whisk for 2 minutes until the mix is thoroughly smooth. Chill for at least 30 minutes, or can be made up to 1 day in advance.

Once the cake is cool, crumble half the gingerbread into the bottom of a trifle or glass bowl.**
Spread half the pudding mixture over the cake, then spread 1 container of Cool Whip over the pudding.

Repeat the layers with the remaining ingredients.

Chill at least 6 hours or overnight.

Garnish with mini gingersnap or gingerbread boy cookies as desired.

Tips:

*If you can't find a gingerbread cake mix, you can substitute a spice cake mix. Add 2 teaspoons ground ginger and replace 2 tablespoons of the vegetable oil called for in the mix with 2 tablespoons molasses. Bake as directed on package.

**You can also make individual servings using wine goblets or cocktail glasses.

HOMEMADE EGGNOG

(Submitted by Kim Davis, from her blog,
Cinnamon and Sugar and a Little Bit of Murder)

Ingredients:

3 cups whole or 2% milk (if you want to be extra decadent, use half and half)
4 eggs
1/2 cup granulated sugar
3/4 teaspoon vanilla
Pinch of salt
Dash of fresh grated nutmeg

Directions:

In a heavy saucepan, whisk the eggs, sugar, vanilla, salt, and nutmeg together. Set aside.

In a microwave-safe bowl, heat the milk in the microwave until hot. Don't boil. I use my Beverage button for this step.

Once the milk is hot, slowly add it to the egg mixture continually whisking to keep the eggs from overheating.

Place saucepan over medium-low heat on the stovetop and, whisking constantly, heat the mixture to 160 degrees (F). If you don't have a thermometer, the mixture should coat the back of a spoon, but for safety, use a thermometer.

Remove eggnog from heat and pour through a strainer. Completely chill the eggnog before using.

Cocoa Kisses
(Submitted by Peggy McAloon)

Ingredients:

3 egg whites
1 cup sugar
1/8 teaspoon salt
1 teaspoon vanilla
3 tablespoons cocoa
3/4 cup chopped nuts

Directions:

Beat egg whites to soft moist peaks; gradually beat in sugar and salt. Continue beating until mixture is thick and glossy; egg whites will stand in peaks.

Fold in vanilla, cocoa, and nuts.

Drop from a teaspoon onto buttered cookie sheet.

Bake in preheated very slow oven (250 degrees) for about 30 minutes or until kisses are partly dry and retain their shapes. Remove from pan while hot.

LOIS TALLMAN'S GINGER SNAPS
(Submitted by Deb Kenyon Thom)

Ingredients:

2 eggs
2 cups sugar
1 cup lard, melted
1 cup sorghum (or molasses)
1 teaspoon salt
1 tablespoon baking soda
1 tablespoon vinegar
2 tablespoons ground ginger
4 cups flour (plus more, if needed)

Directions:

Beat eggs, then add sugar, and beat again.

Dissolve soda in vinegar and add to mixture. Add sorghum (or molasses) and stir together.

Add salt and ginger in with flour, and mix together with other ingredients.

Roll the dough into balls the size of hulled walnuts.

Bake at 375 degrees for 10–12 minutes.
*More flour may be needed to make the dough sufficiently stiff.

SANTA'S WHISKERS COOKIES
(Submitted by Nettie Moore of Moore or
Less Cooking Blog)

Prep time: 20 mins
Cook time: 10 mins
Total time: 30 mins
Makes: 5 dozen

Delicious shortbread cookies filled with cherries, wrapped in
toasted coconut

Ingredients:

3/4 cup butter, softened
3/4 cups sugar
1 tablespoon milk
1 teaspoon vanilla
2 cups all-purpose flour
3/4 cup maraschino cherries, drained and finely chopped
1/3 cup finely chopped pecans
3/4 cup coconut

Directions:

In a large mixing bowl, beat butter with an electric mixer on
medium to high speed for 30 seconds.

Add sugar and beat until combined. Keep scraping sides of bowl.

Beat in milk and vanilla until combined.

Beat in flour on low, as long as you can.

Stir in the remaining flour.

Stir in cherries and pecans.

Shape dough into two 8-inch long rolls and roll in the coconut.

Wrap in plastic wrap and place in the refrigerator for 2–24 hours.

Cut into 1/4 inch thick slices and place 1 inch apart on to an ungreased cookie sheet.

Bake at 375 degrees for 10 to 12 minutes, until the edges are golden brown.

Transfer cookies to a wire rack to cool completely.

ANGEL CRISP COOKIES
(Submitted by Peggy McAloon)

Ingredients:

1/2 cup white sugar
1/2 cup brown sugar
1 teaspoon vanilla
2 cups flour
1 cup shortening
1 teaspoon soda
1 egg
1/2 teaspoon salt

Directions:

Combine all ingredients and roll into balls.

Dip half of the ball on the top side into cold water and then sugar.

Place sugar side up on cookie sheet.

Bake at 375 degrees 9-12 minutes.

Press down the center with a finger and add candied cherry or colored icing.

KOURABIEDES
(Submitted by Elizabeth Christy)

(Greek butter cakes)

Ingredients:

2 1/4 cups flour
1/2 pound margarine or butter
3/4 cup confectioners' sugar
3/4 tablespoon brandy
1/4 teaspoon almond extract
A pinch to 1/4 teaspoon ground cloves

Directions:

Cream together butter and sifted sugar up to 15 minutes.

Sift flour into mix gradually.

Add brandy, almond extract, and cloves and mix well.

Let dough stand in refrigerator for 30 minutes.

Shape into small diamonds about 2 inches by 1 1/2 inches.

Place on ungreased cookie sheets.

Bake at 350 degrees for 20 minutes or until cakes are sandy or light brown.

Cool and place in tin or plastic container.

Sift generously with confectioners' sugar.

KITCHEN-SINK COOKIES
(Submitted by Cynthia Blain)

Prep: 20 minutes Total: 35 minutes, plus cooling

These cookies are chewy and rich, sweet and nutty. Dried apricots or dates also work well. For a tropical variation, substitute sweetened shredded coconut for the oats. Keep up to 3 days in an airtight container at room temperature. Makes 24.

Ingredients:

2 1/2 cups all-purpose flour (spooned and leveled)
1 teaspoon salt
1 teaspoon baking powder
1/2 teaspoon baking soda
1 cup (2 sticks) unsalted butter, room temperature
1 cup packed light-brown sugar
1 1/2 teaspoons light corn syrup
1 tablespoon pure vanilla extract
2 large eggs
1 cup semisweet chocolate chunks
1/2 cup raisins
1/2 cup chopped pecans
1/2 cup old-fashioned rolled oats (not quick-cooking)

Directions:

Preheat oven to 375 degrees. Line two large baking sheets with parchment paper; set aside.

In a large bowl, whisk together flour, salt, baking powder, and baking soda; set aside.

Using an electric mixer, beat together butter, sugar, corn syrup, and vanilla until light and fluffy. Beat in eggs, one at a time, until well incorporated. Gradually beat flour mixture into butter mixture just until combined.

With a rubber spatula, fold in chocolate chunks, raisins, pecans, and oats.

Drop 2-inch balls of dough, spaced 2 inches apart, onto prepared baking sheets. Flatten dough balls slightly. Bake 12 to 16 minutes, or until cookies are lightly browned, rotating sheets halfway through.

Cool 5 minutes on sheets; transfer to a wire rack to cool completely.

GINGER ORANGE COOKIES
(Submitted by Cynthia Blain)

This classic orange sable dough produces cookies with a remarkably delicate texture—they crumble the minute they're in your mouth.

Ingredients:

Makes about 1 1/2 pounds.
1 1/4 cups whole blanched almonds
1 cup confectioners' sugar
3/4 cup (1 1/2 sticks) unsalted butter
3 tablespoons finely grated (2 to 3 oranges) orange zest
1 large egg
1 tablespoon freshly squeezed lemon juice
1 1/2 cups all-purpose flour
6 ounces crystallized ginger, finely chopped (about 1 cup)

Directions:

Place almonds and sugar in the bowl of a food processor. Process until the mixture resembles coarse cornmeal, and set aside.

Place butter and orange zest in the bowl of an electric mixer fitted with the paddle attachment. Beat on medium speed until white and fluffy, 2 to 3 minutes.

On low speed, add the almond mixture, and beat until combined, 10 to 15 seconds. Add egg and lemon juice, and combine. Add flour, and beat until combined.

Wrap in plastic; store, refrigerated, up to 1 week, or freeze up to 3 months. Chill this soft dough very well so it holds its shape when rolled in the ginger.

Place two 12-by-16-inch pieces of parchment on a work surface. Divide dough in half and form each half into a rough log on parchment. Fold parchment over dough; using a ruler, roll and press dough into a 1 1/2-inch cylinder. Wrap. Chill at least 3 hours.

Heat oven to 350 degrees.

Line two baking sheets with parchment. Spread crystallized ginger on a work surface. Unwrap logs; roll in ginger to coat. Cut logs into 1/4-inch-thick rounds and place on sheets, spaced 2 inches apart.

Bake until edges turn slightly golden, about 15 minutes. Transfer cookies to a wire rack to cool. Bake or freeze remaining dough. Store in an airtight container up to 2 weeks.

CHRISTMAS SWIRL FUDGE
(Submitted by Lenda Burns)

Prep: 10 Min.
Total time: 1 HR 10 Min.
Makes: 64

Ingredients:

1 bag (12 oz) white vanilla baking chips (2 cups)
1 container vanilla frosting
Green and red gel food colors

Directions:

Line 8-inch square pan with foil, leaving foil overhanging at 2 opposite sides of pan; spray foil with cooking spray.

In large microwavable bowl, microwave white chips uncovered on High 1 minute. Spoon frosting over chips. Microwave on High 30 seconds; stir. If necessary, continue to microwave in 15-second increments until mixture can be stirred smooth.

Place 3/4 cup fudge mixture into each of 2 small bowls, leaving remaining untinted fudge mixture in bowl. Tint 1 bowl green and 1 bowl red by stirring in each food color to desired color.

Drop heaping tablespoons of green, red, and white fudge mixture in bottom of pan to create random pattern. Pull table knife through layers for marbled design. Refrigerate uncovered until set, about 1 hour.

Remove from pan by lifting foil; peel foil away. Cut into 8 rows by 8 rows. Store covered in refrigerator.

GRANDMA'S KRINGLES

(Submitted by Mary Brockhoff)

Ingredients:

1 lb. butter
1 egg
1 1/4 cups sugar
1 teaspoon almond extract
3 1/2 cups flour

Directions:

Work butter until creamy. Add beaten egg.

Add sugar, almond extract, and flour.

Mix and drop by spoonful on baking sheet. Bake at 500 degrees for a couple of minutes.

Vegan Sugar Cookies
(Submitted by Megan Rivers)

Ingredients:

2 Tablespoons ground flaxseed
1/4 cup nondairy milk (I used Almond Milk or Cashew Milk)
2 1/2 cup sugar
3/4 cup vegan butter (I use Earth Balance)
1 teaspoon vanilla extract
3 cups + 2 Tablespoons flour
2 teaspoons baking powder
1/2 teaspoon salt

Directions:

Mix the ground flaxseed and milk in a small bowl, set aside.

In a large mixing bowl, mix together the sugar and butter with a hand mixer until fluffy.

Add vanilla extract and the flaxseed/milk mixture to the bowl. Mix until blended.

Sift the flour, baking powder, and salt into the bowl and mix using a hand mixer until blended.

Roll the dough into a log-shape. Use parchment or wax paper to help the dough keep its shape and refrigerate for one hour. NOTE: You do not have to roll the dough into a log shape, but it is easier to work with.

Once refrigerated, cut dough into cookie sheets. Bake in the oven at 400 degrees for 5-7 minutes or until the edges are golden brown.

MINT-CHOCOLATE MACARONS

(Submitted by Lisa Maliga, from her book,
Baking French Macarons: A Beginner's Guide)

Macaron Shells

Ingredients:

100 grams almond flour
200 grams powdered sugar
3 large egg whites
50 grams finely granulated sugar
¼ teaspoon cream of tartar
1/2 teaspoon natural green powdered colorant

Temperature: 300 degrees Fahrenheit/150 Celsius

Directions:

Line 3 baking sheets with parchment paper or silpats. Double
the baking sheets to prevent browning. Place a template on a
baking sheet and put the silpat or parchment paper over it. You
can have 3 different templates or just one, which you'll remove
after piping each tray. Have a pastry/piping bag with a large
round tip ready before you begin.

Sift powdered sugar with the almond flour. Whisk to make sure
it's fully blended.

In a stainless steel or glass bowl, beat the egg whites at a low speed
until foamy like a bubble bath before adding the cream of tartar.
Then add granulated sugar in 3 batches. Increase the speed of
your mixer. When finished, the mixture should have stiff peaks.

Add powdered colorant to the flour sugar mixture and then
add half the flour/sugar mixture to the meringue. Fold until the
mixture comes together, scraping the sides and flip batter over.

The batter will be very thick. When the sugar/flour mixture is blended, the batter will be easier to mix and will look shiny. Lift the spatula and note if the batter falls in ribbons from the spatula. Another test is to write the number 8 with the batter.

Scoop batter into piping bag with your spatula. Twist the top of the bag and untwist the bottom, gently pushing the just-poured batter toward the bottom. This removes any excess air.

Pipe batter on the parchment or silpat-lined baking sheets in 1.5-inch circles. Keep the batter just inside circles if using a template.

Rap baking sheet several times on the counter. This will further flatten the macarons, and remove air bubbles. Place a towel on the counter to lessen the noise!

Preheat oven to 300 degrees Fahrenheit/150 Celsius.
Allow macarons to sit for 30-60 minutes until a film forms. Lightly touch a macaron shell and if no batter clings to your finger then it's dry and ready to be baked.

Bake for approximately 20 minutes. Use either the center rack or the one just below it. After about 10 minutes, rotate the tray. The tops should be firm and glossy and the bottoms of the shells should have formed feet or frills at the bottom. When done, the cookies can easily be removed from the parchment or silpat.

Remove from oven and gently slide the parchment or silpat onto a cooling rack. The shells should be cool enough to remove after 10 minutes.

Place macaron shells on a wax paper covered surface for filling. Match the closest sized shells together. For filling your macarons, use a piping bag and the tip size/style is your choice. Don't overfill the shells.

CHOCOLATE-MINT GANACHE FILLING

(Submitted by Lisa Maliga, from her book,
Baking French Macarons: A Beginner's Guide)

Macaron Filling

Ingredients:

4 ounces heavy cream [120 grams]
4 ounces mint chocolate [120 grams]
1 teaspoon vanilla bean paste
½ teaspoon peppermint extract or a few drops peppermint
essential oil

Directions:

Chop up the chocolate and place in a medium glass bowl. Put
heavy cream in a glass container and set microwave timer for
50 seconds. It should be on the verge of boiling. Pour hot cream
over chocolate chunks that are in a glass bowl. Whisk both
ingredients together a few times. Add the vanilla bean paste and
peppermint EO. Cover with cling wrap and let sit overnight. The
next day, mix once more and spoon into a piping bag.

EASY COOKIES
(Submitted by Shelia Hall)

Ingredients:

1 box cake mix (any flavor)
1 box instant pudding mix (any flavor)
1 egg
1 cup oil

Directions:

Mix all ingredients together and roll into 1 inch balls.

Place 2" apart on a greased cookie sheet.

Bake at 325 degrees for 10 minutes or until golden brown.

KHRUSTYKY

(Submitted by Cynthia Blain)

Also called "Ears," this Ukranian pastry is light and crunchy. Really easy to prepare and makes a HUGE batch.

Ingredients:

2 eggs
3 egg yolks
2 tablespoons sugar
1 tablespoon rich cream
2 tablespoons rum or brandy (Or 1 teaspoon of rum, almond or pure vanilla flavoring)
1/2 teaspoon salt
1 cup plus 2 tablespoons sifted flour
Oil or shortening for deep frying

Directions:

Beat the eggs and egg yolks together until light in color.

Beat in sugar, rum or brandy (or extract), cream, and salt.

Stir in the flour. This dough should be soft. Cover and let rest for 10 minutes.

Roll out small amounts of dough at a time, with LOTS of flour on your rolling surface, put flour on top of the dough and on your rolling pin (this dough is very sticky otherwise). Roll to 1/8-inch or thinner. Keep the unused dough covered to prevent drying out.

Cut the dough into long strips, about 1 1/4-inches wide. Then further cut the strips into 2 1/2 or 3-inch segments, diagonally (they will look like 2 1/2-inch long and 1 1/4-inch wide diamonds.) Make a slit in the center (about 1/2-inch long in the middle, lengthwise...) Grasp the bottom tail of the Khrustyky, put it through the slit in the middle, and pull it gently back down to the bottom (this will form a twist in the dough). Continue to do this to each piece of dough. (I roll out a small portion, cut and form my Khrustyky, and set them on a plate. Once my small bit of dough that I've rolled out is all used up, I fry these in the deep fryer before moving on to another piece of dough to roll and cut).

Deep-fry a few at a time in oil at 375 degrees F until light brown. These puff up as you fry them, making a delectable treat. Drain on paper towels. Sprinkle with confectioner's sugar.

PEANUT BRITTLE
(Submitted by Olivine Kenyon)

*Pre-grease a cookie sheet

Ingredients:

1 cup sugar
1 cup raw peanuts
3/4 cup white Karo syrup
1/4 teaspoon salt
1 teaspoon baking soda

Directions:

Put sugar, syrup, and peanuts in pan, mix well and cook to a light golden color. Add salt and stir well.

Turn off burner, put in soda, stir about 15-25 seconds and dump quickly on well-greased cookie sheet.

Tip all corners of sheet and allow candy to spread all on its own. *This last process must be done very quickly!

Cool fast and eat. To break up bang cookie sheet on countertop!

Swedish Coconut Cookies
(Submitted by Nettie Moore)

Prep time: 35 mins
Cook time: 10 mins
Total time: 45 mins
Makes: 72 cookies

Ingredients:

3 1/2 cups flour
2 cups sugar
2 cups butter, softened
1 tablespoon baking powder

1 teaspoon baking soda
1 teaspoon vanilla
1 cup sweetened flaked coconut

Directions:

Combine all ingredients except coconut in large bowl.

Beat at low speed with a hand mixer, scraping bowl often, until well mixed.

Stir in coconut.

Divide dough in half; shape each half into a 12x2-inch log.

Wrap each log in plastic food wrap; refrigerate for at least 2 hours until firm.

Heat oven to 350°F.

Cut logs into 1/4-inch slices.

Place 2 inches apart onto parchment lined cookie sheets.

Bake 10-14 minutes or until edges are lightly browned.

Cool 1 minute on cookie sheet; remove to cooling rack.

Acknowledgments

The Christmas wishes, hopes, and good cheer in *Gingerbread at Moonglow* may appear to be a result of Mist's own unique magic, but in reality, many contributed to this story. Much gratitude goes to Elizabeth Christy for her exceptional developmental and editing expertise. Keri Knutson of Alchemy Book Covers deserves credit for cover design, as well as Richard Houston for eBook formatting, and Tim Renfrow of Book Design and More for print formatting. Beta readers Louise Martens, Jay Garner, Karen Putnam, and Carol Anderson are due a round of applause for their plot insight, with additional thanks to Carol for proofreading.

The townsfolk of Timberton always trade a few holiday treats, thanks to Betty's annual cookie exchange. Heartfelt thanks go to Kim Davis and her blog, Cinnamon and Sugar and a Little Bit of Murder, Nettie Moore and her blog, Moore or Less Baking, Cynthia Blain, Lenda Burns, Megan Rivers, Mary Brockhoff, Peggy McAloon, Deb Kenyon Thom, Olivine Kenyon, Lois Tallman, Shelia Hall, Elizabeth Christy, and Lisa Maliga and her book, Baking French Macarons: A Beginner's Guide, for providing recipes for this year's delicious goodies. Enjoy!

RECIPE NOTES

Recipe Notes

RECIPE NOTES

RECIPE NOTES

RECIPE NOTES

RECIPE NOTES

Lightning Source UK Ltd.
Milton Keynes UK
UKHW011010070223
416609UK00006B/1621